noir

noir

Edited by Ian Whates

NewCon Press
England

First edition, published in the UK April 2014
by NewCon Press

NCP 066 (hardback)
NCP 067 (softback)

10 9 8 7 6 5 4 3 2 1

ISBN: 978-1-907069-64-2 (hardback)
978-1-907069-65-9 (softback)

Grimm Reaper image copyright © Fanny Honningh
Cover design and layout by Ian Whates

Text layout by Storm Constantine

Contents

Noir
An Introduction

Ian Whates

This all started out as a single simple project, but, as so often happens, the concept evolved. The initial idea was to publish a collection of stories each featuring a femme fatale, but on reflection that seemed too restrictive – I mean it wouldn't take any reader more than a story or two to twig what was going on, and surely that made the rest of the book a little... predictable?

So I had a rethink. Even as the theme metamorphosed submissions were coming in, including some terrific stories, but it became increasingly apparent that there was a problem. My usual approach of 'here's the theme, any shade of genre so long as the story's a cracking one' produced a particularly diverse pool of tales this time around. It would be a nightmare selecting from amongst them and producing a volume that hung together with a definable identity and I ran the risk of ending up with a book that suffered from a split personality.

A similar issue had been resolved once before when I divided the all women author *Myth-Understandings* into two sections: *Myth* (the more mythological, fantastical tales) and *Understandings* (the more SF-nal pieces). This time, things refused to fall into place so neatly. By now the theme had moved away from the original femme fatale to a broader brief, but separating submissions along genre lines failed to solve anything.

Only when I started to appreciate that what I had here was *two* books, thematically linked but each with their own identity, did meaningful progress ensue. Once that penny dropped, the project moved forward, swiftly attaining a momentum of its own.

Noir features the usual mix of authors familiar to regular NewCon readers and those who may not be. Marie O'Regan and Paul Kane are established writers of dark fiction and horror who both had stories in *Hauntings* and make a welcome return here, as does Paul Graham Raven, who featured in *Fables from the Fountain*. Adam Roberts' work has featured frequently in NewCon titles and will doubtless do so again. Donna Scott, too, has appeared in previous books (*The Bitten Word* and *Shoes, Ships and Cadavers*). Like Donna, Emma Coleman (*Dark Currents*) is a fellow member of the Northampton SF Writers Group, and when she sent me "The Treehouse", seeking my opinion ahead of possible workshopping, I instantly snapped it up for *Noir*.

I owe a debt of thanks to friends among the writing fraternity for introducing me to many of the book's newer voices. Paula Wakefield submitted her piece at the urging of Storm Constantine, while Tricia Sullivan first alerted me to the work of Alex Dally MacFarlane and Benjanun Sriduangkaew (who features in sister volume *La Femme*) and a recommendation by Dave Hutchinson brought Simon Kurt Unsworth's writing to my attention. I rate Emma (E.J.) Swift as one of the most exciting voices to emerge on the British SF scene for a while, and when I first met her at a London party to celebrate Chris Priest's birthday, I had no hesitation in asking her to submit. Jay Caselberg and I found ourselves sitting next to each other at the launch of the *End of the Road* anthology, which we both have stories in, during World Fantasycon in Brighton. How could I not? James Worrad is someone I've known for a while, and I've been delighted to watch his writing career progress. As for Simon Morden, well, a three-time winner of the Philip K Dick Award, isn't it about time he featured in a NewCon title?

There we have it, *Noir*: thirteen stories that dance around genre boundaries but are linked by a sense of foreboding, a prickly itch that will unsettle and leave you with the impression of something sinister lurking just beyond the reach of awareness…

Ian Whates
Cambridgeshire
February 2012

The Crepuscular Hunter

EJ Swift

Come in, I say, and tell me everything.

I give them the couch, and whichever overlay will put them at ease. White sand beaches. A meadow strewn with buttercups. Something like that. It's rare to get a client who wants to view the world, or my consulting room, bare. They aren't that sort of people. If they want, they can blink me out of the overlay too, but my experience is that they like to see a person – an avatared person, of course – face to face. They want the nuances of expressions, like that slight crease, subtly sympathetic, between the brows. I've perfected the range.

My role lies somewhere between that of confessor and a personal insurance policy.

Come in, I say. Tell me (with a smile that oozes invitation). Everything. For new clients, I apply my most trustworthy[1] avatar: the professional confidant; friendly and assertive, attractive, but not overtly flirtatious. It usually works. I can tell when they're lying and if they don't tell me everything we won't take them on. It's true there have been exceptions – that the boom in memory deletion services has presented us with some problems – but in the end, most people find it a relief to talk.

We – Fitch & Fetch PR, that is, that's who I work for – rep all sorts. Politicians and princesses, bankers and gangsters, even those charity-shop celebrities feted for no one quite remembers what, but they've clung like gel to the slippery slopes of the ladder; you can't fault them for

---

[1] According to recent Amundsen & Partners™ research: Avatar Optimization for Business Success

tenacity. Yes, we'll rep anyone, so long as they pay and they disclose. It's imperative that we have the unfiltered life story, because in the wrong hands the most innocent of scandals can become a maelstrom. Buried memories must be excavated. Secret files unencrypted. The truth poured out, drop by drop, into my receptive ear.

I'll be honest – not all of it's savoury. Some things I wish I'd never heard. Things that make me feel uncomfortable, nauseous, even question what the hell I'm doing. But the contract is golden. Remember. I must remember this.

Once I've gained the client's trust, my colleague tells them the price of a retainer. Hands spread wide, voice expansive, she emphasizes our brand motto. Reputation, reputation, reputation. It's all about reputation. Our clients are glittering diamonds nursed in cotton wool. All they have to do is sparkle. All we have to do is polish them. I won't tell a lie: I'm good at it.

(These reflections are ephemeral, by the way. Erased upon utterance. Well, you don't think I'd disclose to just anyone, do you?)

At the close of a day's work I go downtown; in person, if I'm incentivised, or by digi, if not, to meet my friend K. We frequent a bar on the seventh level which has evolved through cycles of being hip, and not, and currently resides at a crossroads between the two. It's a place that's never quite certain of who it's for and what it's meant to be. A place that's gone off-message.

Tonight the watering hole is busy, full of rippling digis and avatared flesh, chatter bouncing off coalitions of the two. K is cross and fractious. She's had a troublesome day – implying, but not admitting per se, that she didn't perform as well as expected in the quarterly review – but her mood settles after I procure the usual round of tequila. K declares she doesn't want to talk about work, and in the next sentence moans about how she's misunderstood.

I make noises of agreement until she snaps, "Change that bloody avatar, will you?" and I realize I'm still wearing my client-face. I ripple into an edgier version, a Ginkao model. A good avatar is like any good cosmetic: it works with the strengths of your physiognomy and enhances it, and it can't be removed or switched off. Of course, not everyone has the skill to apply their own, and designers are expensive. Like everything in life, you get what you pay for.

Partly to suit the revised avatar and partly for K's benefit, I up the verbal gymnastics, sniping account-to-account about the pitiable figures around us until K laughs – she has a great laugh, K, a beautiful blend of a laugh – and her usual witty flippancy returns. She tells me about a rival firm who have been courting her in private. They want her bad.

"But I can drive the offer up. Those arseholes won't know what's hit them."

I'm glad K's back on form, but as she becomes more jovial I feel my own buoyancy sinking. I'm restless. Inattentive. Small details quickly become a source of annoyance. K's avatar slipping a fraction as she yawns. Crunching on a pip when I bite into a slice of lemon. Now the voice from the digi at the next table is projecting a decibel too high for comfort, shrieking against my eardrums. I've never understood why people can't get their damn audio settings straight.

It's a feeling that's irritatingly familiar. Lately I've been feeling tired. A bit disgusted with it all. I don't know what's up with me. In profile, I have all the hallmarks of satisfaction. A successful career, property and possessions, a trio of alternating lovers – quaint but charming monogamists all, each of whom professes adoration for me alone. And I haven't neglected my physical wellbeing – three times a week I hang upside down in a sauna and let my body be prodded into contortions by the city's leading practitioner in the yogic arts. Pourquoi cette ennui?

This is the thing: I can't ignore a sense of pettiness. A smallness, in the actions of myself and others.

I try to explain this to K and she laughs, the laugh attracting a number of admiring glances, and says I'm having one of my mid-life crises – my many mid-life crises. You were saying all this five years ago, she reminds me. And five years before that –

It's not the same, I say. I knock back a chaser, rolling the sharp tang of the alcohol around my mouth and thinking how even this simple act of surrender insists upon symbolism and is somehow jaded and knowing and contrived. That, I say, was the follies of youth. This time it's different.

K says I should get a dog.

"A dog?"

There are moments when I wonder how K and I are friends. Or perhaps, thinking about it, how I have tolerated her all these years.

"Think of the fun you could have with the do-vatars."

It annoys me that she won't take this seriously, my little moment of tristesse. Perhaps that's the problem. The littleness of it. How can anyone compete in a world where everything must be huge, or vanish? K seems to realize my displeasure and changes the subject.

The crepuscular hunter got another one, she says. Her voice becoming low and mysterious, in the way that voices do when the hunter is mentioned. Just last night.

I nod. I know.

It wasn't one of yours, was it?

No, I say. One of Acton & Singh's.

Well, good, she says. But it's getting worse. That's the second strike this month.

The victim K referred to was high profile, so the incident had gone viral in seconds. Reactions were typical:

commentators using terms like horrific and breach of integrity and disgraceful when what they actually meant was clearly she had it coming and thank fuck it wasn't me (subtext) I'm glad. I was particularly impressed by the phrase breach of integrity, as if the crepuscular hunter were a thing that could have integrity. As if that kind of behavioural conduct could be applied to what was, at heart, a string of digits entered into a machine.

Still, it can be – I have found it – very distressing. Watching the breakdown. The humiliation is so public, so – visceral, I suppose is the word, an old word that I suspect used to mean more than it does today. After the recording had played out a dozen times, and I'd had enough of watching both the incident and the bloom of opinion, what remained in my mind was the idea of something small and grey and distasteful, something that should never be seen with the unadorned eye. As if a previously unclassified sea creature had been plucked squirming from its ocean burrow, and dredged up to the daylight.

To put it another way: the hunter had regurgitated its prey, and had no more use for it.

The victim was female, in her forties, married, with a young child. At first she was of interest. Fascination, even. But quickly enough the watching world decided we had no use for her either. Information is radioactive in its decay: there is only so much the conscious mind can absorb in a given day.

When one of our clients is about to do something, be it a carefully formulated publicity stunt or an error of phenomenal miscalculation (and the latter is not a rare occurrence, not among the clientele we cater to), I analyse the contributing factors and produce a report.

Here's where it could go wrong. Here, or here. This stage, or that. They will love it. They will despise it. They will be ambivalent, in a sophisticated, intellectual but ultimately non-committal manner.

I use rep-maps to depict the viral possibilities and potential deviations from their established reputation. Pre-emptive crisis management, as we call it. Whether or not the events I catastrophize actually come to pass is not my concern – it's someone else's job to work out how to contain the risk, and when necessary, to deal with the fallout.

I'm good, but there are others like me who are also good. When projects conflict it becomes a battle of wits. Us against Acton & Singh. One party creating a situation, the other trying to sabotage it; action, reaction, event, containment. Bloom, contract. Somewhere amidst the competing clouds of our corporations, we weigh up the relative power of word, image, and sound bite. There's a thrill in these titanic clashes. Everything has a weight. Everything has a metric.

The crepuscular hunter was a game-changer.

The crepuscular hunter has no measurements. No agenda that I can see. After the first few incidents, the hunter became a standing item on my reports. That first day, when the client comes in and sits on my couch – imagine the scene, if you will: a release of breath, of tension, the outpouring of history, like a spore, with any flinching on my part hidden under avatar - and a warning.

Have you thought about this? I ask. Have you considered the consequences of...?

They have, of course. A visit from the crepuscular hunter is akin to a tsunami on your wedding day: a natural disaster, unavoidable, annihilating everything.

I never liked her anyway, says K, in the bar. She cups her hands in an emphatic gesture. Not from the start.

I can't be bothered to point out the inaccuracy of this statement. What's the point? K could doctor her feed in the time it takes for me to complete the sentence. Reputation, as

I tell my clients, is ephemeral. And so is identity.

In today's world we have many selves, and two existences. Our physical body, and our digital entity. The two are connected but distinct. Every five minutes there's a new technology, enabling us to hand over another layer of ourselves to the digital entity. Last century it was photographs and emails. This century it's memories and appearance. Next it will be complete consciousness, rendered in the cloud. Inevitable, isn't it? After all, we're all wired by electricity.

Looking at K's hands, a wisp of memory comes to me.

A bird, flying into a room, couldn't find a way out. Pretty thing. Confused and threshing in terror, it was shitting all over the furnishings. We couldn't catch it. (Who was we?) Eventually someone cupped the tiny creature in their hands and put it out of the window. (Who was that?) I laughed. I didn't know if this was the correct reaction.

That memory must be a long time ago, signposted with a locus I've chosen to forget.

Of all our selves it's the shiny ones we choose to display. But imagine if there was something which could reverse that procedure. Imagine the havoc it would wreck.

The crepuscular hunter is two things: an identity thief and a reconstructionist. Before it appeared a few years ago, there were other, less extreme attacks, but not like this. The hunter pecks out identifiers like mites from bark: avatars, communications histories, life-journey and personality auras, everything you have ever projected about yourself. And then it burrows, deep. That ill-advised late-night composition? The footage you thought you'd corrupted beyond recovery? The hunter will find you out: strip you, reboot you, leave you derelict on the trash-strewn beach of the connected world.

The hunter strikes at dusk or dawn; the gap between light and night, when perceptions are hazy and bodies swaddled in dreams. At these times, the perception of self is at its most fluid, and your attention is elsewhere.

What happens in an attack is well-documented. You might be at home, or at work, or walking purposefully to some destination – absorbed in whichever overlay you have chosen to inhabit today. Perhaps there's a shoreline over to your left, with the hiss of the ocean, or a corridor of marble arches overhead, your footsteps echoing, the sunset casting elegant shadows across the floor – whatever it is. Wherever you have chosen to be. There you are, chatting to your mum, or uploading the evidence of last night's (carefully filtered for maximum amusement/irony) shenanigans.

Your physical body is here, your digital entity is there. The reality – the unreality – grows a little dimmer. The details blur. You begin to suspect this is something more than a glitch. It feels virulent. Aggressive. The fabric of the overlay is cracking.

Next moment, your activity is cut short. You try to make central contact but there is no response. You start to shout.

"Hello!"

Nothing comes back. You try again.

"Hello!"

Only a second ago, you were connected, digital. Now you're cut loose in a babbling universe.

This is when the hunter appears.

Most people say it takes the form of a huge owl, the size of a bear. Its head manifests first. A round head with predatory orange eyes, eyes that lock on a level with yours. It has a hooked, machete beak. A beak made for plunging into tissue. Then there are the feet. Each individual talon is the length of a hand, talons which could seize a hold of your shoulders and bear you up and away in a wing-beat.

The hunter glides, moving ever closer towards you. Eyes, relentless, fixed upon yours. You turn and it's there. And there. And there. Whichever way you move the hunter is in front of you. You don't understand – how can it move so fast? A part of you knows that such speed cannot be real – not in the corporeal sense – but you can see it, smell it: an appalling, nauseating smell; what is that? You can hear the rustle of wings as it hovers in front of you, always ahead. You try to duck. To swerve around it – anything to escape.

But the hunter seems to know your intent before you know it yourself.

Most victims collapse at this point, knowing what is coming, not knowing how it will pan out, brain-blank with panic. There's a rushing in your ears. Your heart, hammering. You have never felt terror like this.

The hunter settles gently upon you. You tell yourself, this isn't real, but you can feel its weight. The press of each talon into the clothes on your back. When it reaches your head you start to sob uncontrollably. The talons engage.

The hunter begins to peel you.

That's how victims describe it.

K says she didn't watch last night's attack, but I suspect she's lying. It's funny how even the most highly developed avatars have moments of transparency. There's always an undercurrent of glee when the hunter takes someone. Wanting to see what's left. To examine the nakedness on display, judge it and feel better.

And despite the horror, despite my own revulsion, I can't withhold a certain admiration for the hunter – it's thoroughness, the commitment to obliteration, is in its own way a form of art. But condemnation of the crepuscular hunter is in vogue at the moment. K is clearly adopting this narrative, and who can blame her?

K replenishes our glasses, although I am ready to go home. She senses me flagging. The night is in its infancy, she says. Come now. To be rich and young and inebriate in the city! What more can you desire?

What is young? I ask.

Oh, we've reached the philosophical stage of the evening, have we?

I tell her it was a rhetorical question.

K says my rhetoric grows ever more alarming. To consider the meaning of youth, she says, is to leap with open arms into the abyss.

I ask: what is in the abyss?

K says she doesn't know, probably the crepuscular hunter lives there, with its mates. A parliament of hunters, she says. Just waiting for you.

When a live hunt is imminent a little icon appears at the edge of your enhanced-vision. A pair of round orange eyes, blinking steadily. Open, shut. Open, shut. Yes. Or no. Yes. Or no.

Yes?

If you accept the invitation, you watch the feed there and then.

When it's relayed to the world there is no evidence of the hunter. You see the victim going about their day, lips moving in open conversation, or the eyelash-droop of an upload. Unaware of what's coming. With no warning, they convulse into tremors. Next thing you know they're on the floor, howling as if in terrible pain and flailing against an invisible thing.

As the hunter begins its reconfiguration, the layers of its victims – all those polished shining selves – begin to vanish. Other things swirl to the surface. Internet histories. Medical records. Messages composed but never sent. Memories entrusted to secure banks: all those humiliations and betrayals best forgotten but not quite deleted. It never fails to astonish me how much we record, scattering our footprint across the sky like a comet. And from this debris, the hunter sculpts other stories. Other, lesser, selves.

Its work completed, the hunter leaves the body of its victim whimpering on the floor. Time to switch off, mesdames et messieurs.

It happened once to one of our clients. We had a remedial plan in place, but nothing worked. As I knew from our initial interview, this particular individual had something of a shady past, and I wasn't sorry the hunter had got to him.

Honestly? I felt he had it coming.

Some people just do.

Not everyone.

Back home that night, I kick off my shoes and look out over the city, unenhanced, bare. Clusters of granite-grey buildings, bridges and overpasses, neon advertisements, blinking lights. I wonder, do all cities look the same in the end? It's prettier with the overlay, of course, but without has a rough, raw, different beauty. I switch the overlay on, then off again. The differences are subtle, but unmistakeable. Like the application of a tinted gauze, the overlay gives the illusion of timelessness: the picture of a city with possibility. Where things – things which mean something – still might happen.

Once again I'm conscious of my peculiar state of mind. What am I turning into, some kind of retrotech desperate for affirmation?

Meaning is an illusory as everything else.

I lie back on the couch, switch off the star-overlay and stare up at the ceiling, at once very low and close and claustrophobic, and I look at the cracks in the paint. I want to be closer. I stand on the couch and trace my fingertip along them, feel the rough edges, see the flakes come away on my skin. I wonder why anyone bothered to paint, when nobody sees it. The paint. I think about the person who did the painting and wonder who they are and what they were seeing as they painted, the paint or something else to alleviate the boredom of applying the paint. When I lie back down again, I think I see two orange eyes in a corner of the ceiling. My heart flutters.

Is it?

I wait for the eyes to grow larger, but the hunter does not come. It's only my imagination. Lying here, I can understand the lure of those cults who feel compelled to yield themselves to the hunter as contemporary sacrifices. I think about what would happen if the hunter came for me.

It might find a few things. No weird fetishes or shocking addictions. It's not like that. But I have secrets, of course. Things I wouldn't want exposed.

I consider inviting one of the trio of lovers to talk some filth, but on second thoughts decide I haven't the energy for intimacy and I bring myself off instead.

Over a succession of sleepless nights I wander around the only place the crepuscular hunter couldn't reach: the vault of my memory, a castle. At one point I thought about having some of the unwanted ones surgically removed, or even purchasing some implants, but I know not to entrust my secrets to anyone else – who better? In a room, somewhere in the world, there's a person linked in to those databases, running statistics on the extractions, driving data.

Instead, I practice the method of loci, an old and thoroughly-tested technique. My memories live within the recesses of my brain, in my physical body. But I don't have to recall them unless I want to.

Imagine a place. It must be a large place, a street or a building with corridors and stairways and, if there are things to be forgotten, the chance to get lost. Like a castle. Each memory has a locus: a signpost. Find the locus, retrieve the memory.

Where I grew up is here, locked away in one room. The bird in the room is here. There's a quiet solace in walking the castle's high-ceilinged, grandiose old spaces. Climbing stairs, pacing the corridors, touching my fingers to the rows of doors where the memories dwell. It's calming.

I'm tired now, circadian rhythms winding down. Sleep at last.

In an endeavour to combat my recent and fucking weird[2] moroseness, I take up running. I acquire the requisite avatar, music and overlays, and input an attainable route for beginners. The outdoor city is hostile at this time of year, and the first gasp of sub-zero air feels like a physical assault. I quickly discover I have no stamina. As I wheeze around the course my breath mists and my fingers turn numb.

This is torture.

I return to the flat vowing never to undertake such an irresponsible activity again. That evening I mention it casually to K. She taunts me:

"You're turning into one of those retrotech misanthropists. There's communes, you know."

She seems annoyed, as though I've committed a betrayal. I like provoking her. It occurs to me that the longer the run, the more I can irritate K.

After a while I switch off the overlays and run through the city bare. Noticing things. Noticing people. People who can't afford avatars, drab and ugly alongside their augmented cousins. Avatared or not, everyone looks different from this side.

One day I'm running and an alert pops up eye-right and I see the hunter has struck again, and I scan and huff and run and speed-watch the feed. There is something different about this one. The victim is not high profile, and they are not attached to anyone of note. This is an ordinary person with an ordinary life.

The thing that is strange is that the hunter has taken almost nothing.

It reminds me of what happened with Bo Ziyi, and I feel a tingle of something then. Something like alarm. A sense that the hunter is overstepping the mark.

---

2 K™, Tuesday night, 01:15h

Bo Ziyi fell prey to the hunter two, maybe three years into its campaign. The hunter came for her, but Bo had no layers, no artifice. There was nothing to take or reveal. Bo after the hunter was the same as Bo before the hunter.

At first Bo was lauded. How avant garde, to walk the streets bare-faced, sans avatar. To have nothing to conceal. To choose to conceal nothing. How – revolutionary. The media went to investigate how Bo survived. I followed the story closely – it was, truly, fascinating. But after a while, there was a subtle shift in the media's perception of Bo. When you meet someone, you assume that what you are seeing is a certain presentation, a filter. Bo was not doing that. With Bo, what you saw was what you got. And that, in its way, was a deception in its own right: Bo, by being herself, was pretending to be someone she was not.

After that others weighed in and Bo's life took a turn for the worse. It was catastrophic. If I was rep-mapping her, the projection would look like a drop of ink in clear water. At first the ink is compact, held in a moment of suspension where it is still its own entity. Tendrils unravel; it begins to diffuse. Before you know it, the water is another colour entirely.

Bo moved cities. She applied heavy avatars for protection, changing her face weekly, daily, but someone always tracked her down.

Perhaps that was when my questions first started. I'd always had that peculiar affinity, even admiration, for the hunter – a sense that it was doing something that, whilst uncomfortable, had some angle of morality. But there was nothing moral about what had happened to Bo. Bo's life was over. She had jumped off a bridge overlooking a superway. Her suicide was filmed from multiple angles and a fleet of news drones from the air.

There was a time when you could walk anywhere on the globe and brush your footprints clean behind you, and no one would ever know where you had been or why. No trail but that of your own private memories. People try so fiercely to imprint themselves upon the world, and yet the lives and selves we would choose to have remembered are unlikely to be those which endure.

Of course, I can't say that to our clients. How could I?

Bo Ziyi's suicide became one of the most-watched pieces of footage of all time.

I find I have stopped in the street, thinking about Bo Yiyi and this fresh, oddly similar attack. Almost like a message. I stand, hands on hips, panting, aware of the winter chill on my eyeballs and cheeks. People walk past, avatared, absorbed in the invisible world, oblivious to me, to the city, the clouded sky, the glimmer of frost underfoot. It seems to me that patterns are forming, if I can only understand them. My restlessness, a sense that the world is at once too small and too large, the actions of the hunter, all bound up in some inexplicable sequence. I need to do something. I want to say to the hunter, enough! You've had your fill.

And that's when the idea comes to me.

To lay a trap.

It's mad of course, but the more I think about it, the more I find I can't let the idea go. As if all the ennui of the last few months has been preparation for precisely this moment of enlightenment. The crepuscular hunter has always intrigued me. How does it do what it does? Who is behind it, pulling the strings? I have to know.

I run some metrics on the hunter's victims, but the only pattern is that there is no pattern. They are often, but not always, high profile characters. They have no common interests or habits that I can discern.

Despite the complexities of the target, my plan for the trap is simple. I set up a number of fake accounts which will replicate exponentially. If the hunter is a set of algorithms then it has no means of distinguishing between an actual person and a digital entity. Sooner or later, it will hit upon one of my fakes, and my fake will route back to me.

I meet K in the bar and we drink tequila and I tell her how many kilometres I have conquered this week, and that it gives me a feeling of intense exhilaration. This is (mostly) a lie – every run makes me feel like vomiting. Nonetheless there's something, an addiction I can't deny, that takes me back again and again to the naked streets, and the more my obsession with the hunter grows, the more I want to run. K looks disgusted at my antics. I wonder if she'll give up on me soon.

About my trap, I say nothing. I have no clear answer for why I am doing this, only a compulsion which must be answered.

Weeks pass. I run at dawn. I run at dusk. I drink at night. I tell my clients: "Come in, sit down, and tell me everything." I congratulate K on her new contract, an astral ascension for my friend. I'm glad for you, I say, and I really think I am. K is moaning more than ever so she must be happy. I keep tabs on my expanding digital bait, but the crepuscular hunter does not come.

In the last week the hunter has upped its campaign. It took five victims: two at dawn, and three at dusk. A retired actress, a memory clinic technician, an entrepreneur, an energy exec, a trainee nurse. Almost as if it knows what I'm doing. I begin to wonder if the hunter has some intuition I did not previously suspect, if the virus might be more human than the binary construct I have in mind.

The tide has changed; there is an undercurrent of anger now when the hunter is mentioned. Newsreaders talk of a growing police investigation. They employ words like prosecution and sentence, but I know the hunter is too clever for them. They show images of the victims. They say there is a warped mind behind the hunter.

The hunter's victims have the eyes of the haunted. They relay their experiences, but they cannot look you in the face, even under avatar.

It does make me feel rather sick.

When it finally happens I am running. Has the hunter found me or one of my decoys? It happens too fast to tell.

The eyes appear first.

There's a second of dread, the heart-pump rush of adrenaline to my aid, but it's all right, I've prepared for this moment. I know what to do. Instantly, I disconnect everything from my digital canvas – my very clean digital canvas. I stop where I am in the street and internally take flight, retreating into the safety of my castle.

The hunter can't get to me here. As long as I stay inside, within its walls, I'm impregnable.

Inside it's cool and echoey and familiar. I climb the main stairs, my hand gliding along the rail, my feet sinking into the soft woven carpet. I'm barefoot – I'm always barefoot in here. Your feet are connected to every other part of your body, so I think it aids the loci. I pass the doors where my memories are stored. I touch my hand to the woodwork, acknowledging what lies within.

A bird, flying into a room.

My first kiss. Cringeworthy, but with a certain nostalgia attached.

Further back. Former lives, former selves. The place I grew up –

Moving on.

What I'm banking on is that somewhere in here there's a back door. I can slip out the other side, and when I return to the real virtual world I will have evaded the hunter successfully. This is my gamble.

I'm on the third floor when I notice a door I've never seen before. A shrunken green Alice In Wonderland style door no higher than my hip. Curious, I turn the handle, and meet with resistance. There's no lock, though – the door seems to have warped in its frame. I shove harder and it springs open. I duck through into an unfamiliar corridor. What the hell is this?

I've entered a part of my palace that's alive, and foreign to the front of my brain. Grasses have grown tall through cracks in the walls and floors. The blades rustle against my fingers, dry and sharp edged, plumes of dust lifting as I walk through. This is proper fairytale stuff. Empty, of course, like the rest of the palace, and it occurs to me now that it's a strange thing to create a place that is unpopulated, without even a guide to show me around. Why didn't I locate a guide? No matter, I sense I'm closer now. To the back door, I assume. There is a purpose in my feet, even as I pause, curious, to touch things, feeling the crumbling texture of the walls and the soft stickiness of cobwebs.

I reach the end of the corridor. There is only one door. It has an old-fashioned lock located at about waist height. I slip my hand into my back pocket as though I've done this a thousand times before and my fingers fold around a large metal key, cold against my palm. When I fit it to the lock it turns easily. I open the door, and realize my colossal miscalculation.

Inside is the crepuscular hunter.

Its eyes, huge, fixate upon me. Before I can think, move, do anything, I'm enfolded in suffocating feathers and in the moments the hunter has me within its wingspan I hear the door slam closed. I'm inside with it. There's no escape. The fear takes me like immersion in icy water: everywhere, all around – nothing but fear to feel – and I have no oxygen to breathe.

The crepuscular hunter is too large for the room. It is larger than me, three, four times my size.

There is an appalling stench in the room. At first I think it is the hunter itself, and then I realize the floor at the back of the room is covered in pellets. There's a familiarity to the pellets; the hints of shapes that might be limbs, twisted and crushed, here and there the impression of a face. Pile upon pile of them. With a nauseating rush of horror I realize that the pellets are identities. Chewed up and spat out, rotting where the crepuscular hunter left them.

The crepuscular hunter opens its beak wide and screeches. I can see its yawning throat, wet and pinkish, the ridges that line each side of its terrible beak, the slippery tunnel down which I would slide. I realize that this is what the hunter is ready to do to me.

But there is something else in the room.

Someone else.

A slight figure, skulking in the shadows. The figure seems in no rush to come out, which is not surprising considering the terrifying apparition before me, but it is clearly interested in what is going on in front of the crepuscular hunter. The hunter's wings thresh between us, stirring hot rank air around the room. The avian thing – I can't call it an owl, it's a monster – squawks again. Between outstretched feathers I glimpse the skulking one. I think it's a female.

The hunter has not struck and it occurs to me that the figure, on the other side, has some kind of power over it.

"Hey!" I shout, but my voice comes out thin and terrified. I try again.

"Hey!"

The figure leans out from beyond one wing, but she is still in the gloom, and I cannot see her face.

"Yes?"

"Won't you help me?"

"Do you need help?"

"What do you think? I'm about to be eaten!"

The figure slouches forwards.

It takes a few seconds to register what I am seeing, because I haven't seen her face in a very long time. It's an old face. It's lighter and looser and lined. The skin is unaugmented.

I back away, not wanting to acknowledge the truth, and find myself up against the door.

What I am seeing is myself.

Or a version of myself – maybe many versions of myself. An older me, anyhow. A memory me. This other self is not just in the shadows, she is shadowy in form, a loose swirling thing that does not quite fit together, and yet moves as a whole.

I meet my eyes, my nose, an upper lip that curls more than I am used to.

"What are you doing here?" I say. I duck as the wing of the hunter slices downwards and its foot scrapes across the floor with a hellish sound. I try to ignore the pounding in my chest that says this cannot be, this is not possible.

I made it this way.

"You're slow today," says my memory self. "I thought better of you."

"You're judgmental today," I say.

I am forced to drop and roll in order to avoid another swipe of a wing.

"Can you ask that thing to stop?"

"Oh – yes."

The swirling parts of my memory self separate and come together like smoke. I can't get a fix on her. The hunter lowers its wings, and its beak clamps shut, although the eyes continue to glare at me.

"You could ask it too, you know," says my memory self. "After all, it does belong to you."

I stare at the crepuscular hunter, which makes a hawking sound in its throat, as if it might disgorge something unspeakable.

"Are you mad?"

"Not mad. Not according to psychiatric definitions. But you've certainly buried me deep. I did wonder why you came here now."

I am beginning to see, and I don't like it. I don't like it at all.

"Tell me."

"Come in, sit down."

I decline, and do not complete the sentence, which evidently amuses my opposite. Parts of the hunter's victims are strewn across the floor. Pieces of smiles and frowns and musculature and augmented skin.

"Who was I, before you?"

"You were nobody."

"Is that so bad?"

"You thought it was."

I think about this.

"But I'm still nobody."

"You can change that," says my memory self. "You can end this. Here and now. All you have to do is walk out of the palace, and open your eyes."

"But –" I don't understand. "The hunter's gone?"

"It's still there."

"So it can get to me."

"I'm afraid you programmed it that way. You wanted it to be completely random, and you wanted yourself to be trackable."

"But –" I feel dense, stupid. Unable to compute what I am hearing. "Why? Why would I do that?"

"You said you felt a kind of pettiness. A smallness in the actions of yourself and others. A certain... ennui."

"That sounds familiar," I say dryly.

"You do tend to go in five year cycles."

"We," I correct.

"We."

The hunter shifts its gigantic feet with those ripping talons. It is growing impatient.

"Is there any way out?" I ask.

"No."

A pause.

"This day might never have come, you know," says my memory self. "That's the beauty of it."

"But it has."

The hunter clicks its beak. This is the moment when I should make any last requests, but my mind is strangely blank – panic I suppose – and the only thing I can think of is running. The streets, the glimmer of frost, the huff of my breath expelled in white clouds.

And then I realize I have been running for a long time, a much longer time than I thought.

"Before it eats you," says my memory self. "Sit down, and I'll tell you everything."

Gross Thousand

Adam Roberts

And Jacob asked him, and said, Tell me, I pray thee, thy name. And he said, Wherefore is it that thou dost ask after my name? And he blessed him there.

[Genesis 32:29]

I emerged from Highgate tube just as a big grey cloud muffled the sun. Light dimmed. Pigeons scurried diagonally upwards, like flustered angels. Out of the depths, I thought. Out of the depths and along the London streets.

It was a twelve minute walk to his building. The doorbell sounded two notes, a falling fifth. He had to come down the stairs to answer; and he led me back up into a first floor conversion. Tidy, smelling of yesterday's cooking and coal-tar soap. It was unostentatiously furnished, except for a positively enormous Wide Screen HD television in the corner of the sitting room. I only realised why he had such an expensive piece of kit afterwards, when transcribing the interview (which I give below, shorn only of its more excessive hesitancies).

He had an unBritish sort of name – Gus Vargtimmen – but he was a British national for all that, and spoke with a low, slow voice tinted with South London. Identifying the precise location of accents is a hobby of mine, and as I spoke to him I tried to place his. Tooting, I thought; perhaps Wandsworth. He made me tea. We sat down. I put the mp3 player on the table between us. I looked at him and asked, "Is it okay I record?"

He nodded. 56 years of age (I knew this from his file). He looked older.

I asked him: "What I'd like is for you to tell me the

nature of your beliefs; I mean, in your own words."

"I've many beliefs," he said. He waited. "I know what you mean," he went on, eventually. "It was Aldridge?"

"Professor Aldridge did tell me about you," I said. "That's true. But I'd like to hear your version of things."

Vargtimmen closed his eyes and opened them again. The motion was just too prolonged to be a blink. "It's odd, you calling it a belief," he said. "That ought to be a straightforward word. Ought to mean what it says. But it never does, does it? You see me sitting here: and you can say *I see you sitting there*. That would all be fine and dindy-dandy. But if you said *I believe I see you sitting there*, it would actually imply that you weren't sure – wouldn't it? Ain't that strange? That asserting your belief actually signals that you weren't entirely *sure* about your belief."

"Mr Vargtimmen," I said.

"Aldridge also had little patience for phee," said Vargtimmen, and sighed. "-*lo*sophy. But, really, I've come to see, there's nothing else of importance in the world. Philosophy—theology – language, ethics and *ont*ology." His eyes drifted to the patch of wall beside me.

"What do you do for a living, Mr Vargtimmen?" I asked.

"Nothing, any more," he replied. "I used to run an off license. The Oddbins, on Peckham Rye, as it happens. But I quit that." He met my gaze. "I quit that. You're thinking: *out with it*. You want me to spill. I'll oblige you."

I waited.

"When I *look* at someone I can see, straight," he said, his gaze slipping away again, to the left, "straight away whether they are going to heaven or hell."

"You mean, after they die?"

"Of course after they die."

I nodded. "So, please – I'm intrigued. I'm wondering how?"

"I don't know how."

"Not how are you able to see this," I said. "Let's leave that aside for a moment. I should have framed my question more carefully. I mean: how can you tell *before* a person dies if they're going to heaven or, the other place? I'll be plainer: let's say you see somebody and they're marked for hell. How do you know they're not going to repent tomorrow and be saved? And if you see someone who's going to heaven –" Vargtimmen's gaze snapped back to meet mine – "well, for all you know that person will commit an unforgiveable sin tomorrow. Do you see?"

"It makes," said Vargtimmen, "no odds. I *see* it. We're all already dead, from the point of view of the end of time."

It's never wholly comfortable conducting a psychiatric interview and hearing the interviewee say something like *we're all already dead*. I reacted the English way. Which is to say, I smiled, and nodded, and spoke quickly, picking up the less threatening element of the statement. "So you're saying you have been gifted a view of the universe from the end of time?"

Vargtimmen put his head a little to one side, as if this question were a new one for him. "No," he replied. "Not that. I'm saying that a person's absolute goodness or depravity, the sum of that person's whole life and spiritual choice, is immanent in them, from the moment they're born. That's got nothing to do with me. That's just the way things are. The only thing is, I can *see* it. And most people can't."

"Have you always been able to do this?" I asked. "Have you always had this – sight?"

His expression shifted minutely; and I could see this question bored him. "No," he said. "It came on me."

"When?"

"Eighteen months ago."

"You've been asked that question before," I noted. "I'm sorry; it must be boring to have to repeat your answers over and over."

"You could say that," he said.

35

"Okay. I'm guessing there are three questions you've been asked a hundred times, by every mental health and social-care professional who has ever interviewed you about your... special sight. Do you mind if I ask all three now, to get them out of the way?"

I could see this was the right way to play him. He sat up in his chair a little. "Let's see if you're right. About which three questions. Fire away."

"Well, I'm thinking one will be: how do people appear to you, so that you can tell which direction their souls are headed? Do the hellbound have a red glow about them? Are the heavenly glittery with white light? Is there a halo over their heads?"

"That's one of the questions," he agreed. "Score one for you. A bonus point, Ms Janissary, if you can guess how I answer."

"I'd assume you say: there's nothing like that. That there's no egregious symbolism about it. I'd assume you'd say: you can just tell."

He grunted. "Pretty much. And the second question?"

"Well," I said, "the second question is probably – can you make the same judgment about yourself?"

He nodded again. "That's number two, exactly. And the answer is: no, I can't. I'm the only person in the world I can't make that judgment of. I look at myself in the mirror, and I'm a blank." He shrugged. "That's just the way it is. But that doesn't matter. It matters not at all. And the third?"

"Well," I said, feeling strangely awkward about this. "I suppose the third most frequently-asked question must be: what about me? Where am *I* going – when I die?"

Vargtimmen looked at me. "That's right," he said. "That's what everybody asks me."

I waited. "And?'

"You really want me to tell you what I see?"

"No," I replied, gravely. "I suppose not. But Aldridge said something about one hundred forty-four thousand?"

"That's the number of the saved," he confirmed.

"You mean – you've seen 144,000 saved people? That's quite a number!" I smiled at him, but he didn't smile back. "And it's Biblical, yes? I mean – I ask because your vision *is* religion-specific."

"The 144,000 figure is in the Bible, yes," he confirmed. "The world will end when the 144,000 who are saved enter into heaven." Then, reciting from memory: "Revelation 14. I heard the number of the sealed, a hundred and forty-four thousand. Then I looked, and behold, on Mount Zion stood the Lamb, and with him 144,000 who had his name and his Father's name written on their foreheads. And they were singing a new song before the throne. No one could learn that song except the 144,000 who had been redeemed from the earth."

"And were you raised as a Christian?"

"I was not," he snapped; but immediately he added. "Christianity is the broader culture in which I have grown up. I assume you're saying something like: oh, if you'd been born in an Islamic culture you'd see things differently. I don't know. I only know what I see."

"It sounds a lot," I said. "Nearly a hundred and fifty thousand people. But I suppose it's not really that big a number."

Something about his expression, or his body language, shifted when I said this. There was a new attentiveness about him. "Go on," he said, speaking slowly.

"What do you mean? Go on –?"

"That's not one of the questions I'm asked," he said. "I mean, it wasn't a question, I know. But it ain't something the people who quiz me *usually* notice."

"The numbers, you mean?" I said. "Really?"

"That's right."

"Well," I said. "Anyone can do the sums. How many people are alive today, and how many have ever lived? Add the numbers together – twenty billion? It's probably a lot more, but let's stick with that for the moment. So if the world ended tomorrow, and God totted up the total numbers, 144,000 out of 20,000,000,000 would be saved." I pulled out my phone and tapped the calculator tab. "That gives any one individual a... 0.00000072 chance of being saved. That's, rounding up, what – a millionth of a percent chance? I can't say I like those odds!"

"You are not a religious person," he said.

"Why do you assume that?"

"You wouldn't rattle that sum off so flippantly if you were. That sum – that... that piece of maths. It's the most profound thing you've ever said in your life. It's the weightiest thing that's ever come out of your mouth."

"Really?"

He didn't reply at first; but then, slowly, he drew himself up in his chair. "Aldridge knew about the number," he said. "The 144,000. But you're the first person I've spoken to who has put two and two together. I mean, I guess it sounds like a lot. Quite a crowd. It means that heaven is a city the size of Reading. But, the rest? The rest? I don't mean to be hard on you. I've only realised myself because I can, you know: see it directly. God created a hundred billion souls, but He did it... I don't know. He did it the same way a squid squirts out millions of eggs knowing only one or two will ever actually get to hatch. Some great squid, skin black and shiny as liquorish, tentacles like dreadlocks. Almost all its eggs will be gobbled up by the monsters of the deep, and so it is with us." He coughed, once, twice, and then slapped his own chest fiercely. "I have stood in the top tier of a football stadium containing twenty thousand people, and looked to see that *none* of them will be saved. I've had that experience over and over and over again. I've been to a hundred football matches, probably more – two hundred, three, I don't know. And do you know how many of the saved I have seen in all those years of attending the biggest crowd-packed stadia? Two. I saw two at a United Blackburn match six years ago. And I saw another – I mean, I'm guessing he was one of the two same guys as earlier – at United-Chelsea. Otherwise, crowds and crowds of people, and all of them damned. Every single one. Hundreds of thousands of people, seen with my own eyes, a drop in the bucket."

"Well," I said, provoking him a little, but doing so tactically (I had a diagnosis to determine, after all); "the maths would suggest that you were lucky to see three! You ought to see one saved person in every million!"

"Every hundred million," he said, in a flat voice.

"Is that – no, you're right. Well then!" I smiled at him. But his face had assumed the repose of melancholy. To chivvy him a little, I asked. "You're a football fan?"

He lifted his face. "No," he said.

"Oh, I would have assumed you followed Manchester United. I was only going to say that my partner is a fanatical Manchester United fan."

"I have been to a great many football matches. I do not like football."

"Then why go?" But I was being dense. "No," I added immediately. "I see. You didn't go because you were interested in the game. You went because you were interested in the crowd."

"I spent three years, three full years, and that was my obsession," he said. "I sought out large crowds. I moved among them. I was searching. I don't need to be there in person, you know; I can watch somebody on TV and see whether they are going to heaven and hell. Newsreaders and weathermen. Children's television presenters and actors and people appearing on game shows. I watched a documentary about World War Two, and saw old black and white footage of the crowds pouring through Trafalgar Square, and do you know how many of them were saved? None at all. I've watched live coverage of scores of mass events: the Pope addressing crowds in St Peter's square and I see nobody to be saved. I watched the Al-Jazeira coverage of the Haj three years running, footage of a crowd so large in motion around the holy place of Mecca that it looks like a fluid – three years, probably millions of people, and do you know how many of them were saved? One."

"A Muslim?"

"Oh I don't know how it works. I don't know the how. I only see. I walk the streets and see crowds flowing into the shops and out again, women pushing buggies with babies in them and the women and the babies are all damned, and will spent forever in hell being punished. I watched the coverage of the royal wedding and not a *single* person there will go to heaven. So, yes, there was a time when I became obsessed with seeking out the saved. I became – depressed." He held out the palms of his hands, as if for me to inspect. "Who wouldn't?"

"How many have you seen?"

"Saved people?" He folded his hands back into his lap. "Four. I've seen eight, but I'm pretty sure the extra four were duplicates, people I'd already seen before. It's hard to be sure when you're looking at a large crowd."

"Did you ever approach any of the saved people you saw?"

He laughed. "I didn't. Those two people I saw at football matches – they were the only ones I've seen in the flesh. And they were part of a huge multitude on the far side of a crammed football stadium. It excited me. Two at once! It was why I kept going back to matches. Maybe I thought there was something special about football. There's not, though. Otherwise – well I've thought: what would I do if I *did* bump into one? What if I were walking down the high street and I saw one of the saved, coming towards me? It's never happened, but what would I do? Would I speak to them – embrace them – assure them of their good fortune? They'd think I was mad." He gave me a quick, though significant, look. "No, I'd have to leave them alone. That was why I stopped crowd-searching. The brute fact of the numbers came home to me. What is the point?"

"You realise," I said, shortly, "that you've inadvertently answered the third of the three most-frequently-asked questions? About me, I mean: about whether I'm personally going to heaven or hell?"

He coughed again. "You did the sums. Your answer is there. And mine too. You wanted to know if I could see where I myself was going. I can't, but I don't need to. It's obvious enough."

I smiled at this, but I'll confess I felt discomforted. I was aware, of course, of the dangers of becoming drawn in to a patient's mania; some insane people can appear not only mild and reasonable (as Vargtimmen certainly did) but strangely persuasive too. I'm not saying I believed him. But there *was* a quality to his quiet, downbeat insistence that was starting to wear away at my natural positivity. "Well I'm sure there's still time for me. To repent, I mean. If I believed in all that. The 144,000 number comes from the Bible, after all. And doesn't the Bible also include all sorts of methods for atoning for your sins so you can go to heaven?"

"Napoleon," he said.

"What about him?"

"He went to hell."

Put like that, so bluntly, it seemed a weirdly brutal thing to say. "Well I suppose he was responsible for many deaths. He started wars, so perhaps that doesn't surprise me."

"You think that's got anything to do with it? Mrs Holbrook-Jackson lives in the flat downstairs, a perfectly innocuous little widow woman, seventy-nine years young. Lived, so far as I can tell, a respectably blameless life. Church of England, housework, kids. She's going to hell. She certainly never started any wars."

"And you're sure about Napoleon," I said, wanting to get the conversation off the neighbour.

"I can read portraits."

"So, not just photographs and TV – paintings too?"

"It depends on the painting. If they were done from life, then yes. It's the same with the telly. I know that Philip Schofield is going to hell, but I get no reading off Peppa Pig."

"Why do you mention Napoleon?"

"Because he is already in hell. Do you think he can repent? Now that he's there, I mean?"

"Can a person repent when they're actually *in* hell? I don't know what the theology is on that one. I'd assume not. By then it's too late, no?"

"It's too late. Once he's dead he can't undo the evil he has done, whatever it is. But this is my point: whether you're in hell in the past or the future is only a sort of optical illusion, predicated upon where you happen to be standing at the time. Standing in 1810, Napoleon might say: *oh there's still time, I can repent, I may not go to hell.* Standing in 2010 we can say: *he's in hell, he missed his chance.* 2010 trumps 1810. And here's the thing: God stands at the end of time. It's all already happened, as far as he's concerned. It doesn't look that way to *us*, but that's a trick of perspective. The actuality is… well, one aspect of the actuality is what I can see. With vanishingly few exceptions, we're all already damned. You. Me. Mrs Holbrook-Jackson. Everyone we've ever met, or known, or loved."

"Well," I said, breezily, putting on a big smile. "At least we won't be lonely down there!"

He shook his head. "Lonely is exactly what we'll be. Desperately alone and in staggering pain and without hope forever."

I was silent for a while. The little light on the mp3 was winking at me; a little red LCD flicking off and on. "Well," I said, eventually; meaning to carry the sentence on with something along the lines of *thank you, that's been very helpful.* But the words didn't seem the right thing to say. I finished my tea.

Outside the afternoon was breezy, sunshiny. I walked briskly along the high street and towards the Tube, my backpack sluing over my left shoulder. I passed the tall windows of the department store along which reflected clouds were sliding smoothly and silently, managing to hurdle the obstacle of the central upright spar without any damage to their reflected integrity. Words sometimes pop into my head, unbidden and apparently at random; and given my training and interests you won't be surprised to hear that I stop, periodically, and jot these words down in a red moleskin notebook I carry just for that purpose. It interests me, and can occasionally yield insight. And *down* I went. As I waited on the cool, neon lit platform of the Northern Line southbound I wrote: *kilter; sunlight; gross; malediction; pigeon.* I put the notebook away. Then the air bunched and pushed against me, and my hair blew back, which of course meant that the train was coming.

The Grimoire

Donna Scott

A grimoire, you say? Oh, yes, I think I can help you as it happens… but let me tell you, they're a devil to track down: the trouble with grimoires is that they are forever disguising themselves as *books*.

I am curious as to how you heard about my little shop. How did you know this would be the right place to look? I agree, yes, we do have the right sort of ambience for them. Nothing plastic about this establishment. Not a whiff of commercialism… nor indeed, much profit. But books, yes, they are always very welcome here.

You know, people might be all kinds of brave around one or two paperbacks, but they can be very intimidated by *lots* of books. Likewise, books dislike lots of people. I feel sorry for the ones in that big bookshop in town – the one with all the cards and mugs and toys on the ground floor and all the books trying to hide upstairs. I've seen them huddling under 'Poetry' thinking no one will ever find them there. And then they get burrowed out and flung on the twofer tables, all face up and prone to greasy fingers. Mind, I don't blame new books for being scared of having their spines broken by careless browsers! – That first *crack* is always the worst – And you'd never see an age-old grimoire settled there, where it's *accessible*. Unlike this place…

Anyway, as I say, grimoires can be tricky things to find, so here, take a chair while I rootle around and try to – *grrr*, good grief this box is heavy – find this thing for you. And I'll tell you about the last person to come in here looking for a grimoire.

I remember it was a gorgeous, sunny day in June last year.

Quite chilly in here, though. I never take these gloves off, you know, except to turn the odd stuck page.

But yes, the woman... the *witch* I should probably say, though she looked nothing like the old hags from the fairy tales. In she came, wearing a white sundress, and I thought to myself, there's someone going to get black dust and cobwebs stuck to them and then complain to me about it. Because she didn't look at all unsure of herself, you know. Well-kept sort of lady, with long brown hair, a bit like that newsreader who does the dancing. I'm always wary of people who come in smiling... Most people who enter a second-hand bookshop will offer no more than a cursory nod before edging their way to the first shadowy alcove out of my line of sight. It's a game, see. I'm supposed to ask them if there's anything particular they're looking for, and then they're supposed to tell me. Then I find the book in question or I don't. Then they are supposed to leave. That's what happens in other shops. Most folks who wander in here have no idea what they're really looking for. But I find what they need.

The woman bade me, "Good morning," in a voice that was rich and honeyed enough to drown an ortolan. I said hello back and asked if there was anything I could do for her, and she said yes...

Now here's where you're probably thinking she mentioned a specifically esoteric sort of title. A *Necronomicon* perhaps, or Volumes 1-6 combined of Conrad Horst; a small volume from the Bibliothèque Bleu; an Agrippa facsimile...

"I'm looking for *The History of Reynard the Foxe*," she said. "Kelmscott Press edition."

I gulped at that. It just so happened that I did have the very book the lady had mentioned. But it was no ordinary book. It was a most beautiful thing, bound in snow-white vellum, tied in ribbons of decaying yellowed silk. Printed by William Morris's own press, with woodcut illustrations by

Burne-Jones and block letters in the manner of ages past; made to be a piece of art, a precious object. The story itself was one taken from Caxton's translation into English of an old Dutch version of the tale of a fox who refuses to go to court in case the Lion King finds out about his crimes against all the other beasts. And being a Kelmscott edition, I knew it was something special; got it in a house clearance a few months before from some old fellow's shelves, and I'd already telephoned the University of Birmingham – they have a lot of Kelmscotts in their Fine Print and Rare Editions Collection. And Frank, the curator, had asked me to pop the book along to him some time for a look – only I'd have to wait for an opportune moment to close the shop. I'd been half-expecting Frank to come to me instead.

"You're not Frank," I said to the lady, stating the obvious. "Did he send you?"

"I'm sorry," she said. "I don't have the faintest idea who you're talking about."

There was something slightly off about the way she spoke. For a second, I couldn't put my finger on it. Was it the slow and deliberate way she had formed the words? The tone of her voice? Was it the fact she was still smiling as if she were advertising hairspray? I suddenly felt very cold, and was thinking of putting my pullover back on, when I realised I was already wearing it.

"I'm sorry too, ma'am," I said. "I don't have any Kelmscotts in at the moment. If it's rare editions you're after, I've got a first edition *Harry Potter and the Philosopher's Stone* newly acquired, about to be showcased on an antique book site, after which I'm expecting it to fly... or if it's late Middle English works you're interested in, I do have a number of Caxton facsimile reprints, including your fox tale, I do believe–"

And then it seemed that the dark had suddenly descended in my little shop, and the smile disappeared from the woman's face, and all the honey from her voice.

"Vellum. Handmade. Kelmscott.," she spat, almost shouting. Quite rude, I thought. But she got worse. After a dramatic sigh of exasperation, she continued: "From the house of Harry Irving, deceased. Would have been in the company of quite a few other books. Let me jog your memory of some of them." Then she began marching round my shelves, pulling books from them and flinging them haphazardly towards my feet. "One book of Fleur Adcock poetry; *Kidnapped* by Robert Louis Stevenson; *The Railway Children* by E Nesbitt; Thomas Babington Macauley's *Lays of Ancient Rome*; *Liber B vel Magi* by Aleister Crowley, and–" she marched over to my cluttered desk and took the top book out of a box on top that I had yet to sort through.

"Great Scott! Stop a second," I said, my hands held up in case she decided to fling that one at me from close range. I was sorely tempted to punch the woman. As I took a step towards her I think she thought I might because she stepped back as if to dodge out of my way, her eyes half-wild still. "Right, stopped throwing my shop around, have we? Good. Okay, let's discuss this like adults. How do you know these books are from this Harry fellow?"

"One *Basic French Cookery Course*," she continued, thrusting her chin up at me as if in challenge. "By master spy thriller writer, Len Deighton, of course. Signed *to Lissy*." She held the book open on the fly, revealing the author's signature."

"How did you–?" I began.

"Know? Because I know these books and they know me. I have grown up with them." She shrugged. "And because the box has *H. Irving House Clearance* written on it in marker pen."

I had to concede that it did.

"So, if you grew up with them, you're his daughter?"

She arched an eyebrow and said haughtily, "No. I was his pupil. And his *lover*."

Feelings along the lines of being scandalised threatened

to surface at that moment, what with Mr Irving having been an old fella, and this woman... well, I struggled to put an age to her. Not a *very* young lady. But I wouldn't say middle-aged either. She was a bit too smooth and glamorous, if you know what I mean? But I put my sense of propriety aside. I mean, I'd spoken to the man's nephew and he said there was no other family left; no one else who might want his stuff. It had all been left to him and he didn't want any of the books. And I'd only given him a hundred for the lot – including the Kelmscott. I had been looking at a tidy profit. I suspected this lady had the same in mind, but did she have any real claim to the books? I didn't think so. She may have recognised a few from the clearance, but really she could have been anybody.

So, I asked her again. "His lover?

"Yes," she replied, holding my gaze, but oh so slightly twitching.

"I nodded to the book in her hand. "Are you Lissy?"

"No."

"Oh," I said. "I'm sorry for your loss." Then I took the book out of her hand and put it back in the box. Which she promptly upended, books scattering all over the desk and floor, mixing up the ones I'd made a note of with ones I hadn't and customer orders ready to go. I clenched my fists, but forced myself to keep them down. What a mess!

I tell you, people who mistreat books will never earn a special favour from me, so as she was shrieking, "Where is it? Where is it?" I abandoned any thought that may have been forming to do a deal with her on the Kelmscott instead of the University.

"I don't have it," I told her again. "Now kindly leave my shop."

This she did, though I had to practically shove her out, with my arms mimicking the blade of a snowplough, as it were. And then, as I sometimes do, I decided to close a few minutes early and get on with my cataloguing and bookwork, as I had quite a lot to do and was feeling too tense to cope with customers. The woman banged on the door for a bit, but she stopped after twenty minutes or so. Just as well the local residents in this area were all out at work, or I'm sure one of them would have telephoned the police...

I apologise, the book I was searching for isn't here after all that. Might be hiding upstairs. Yes, there is an upstairs, but I generally keep the stairway concealed behind that stack of shelves there. I'll just turn the sign round on the door for now, just in case, pop the bar across like so, and you can follow me up.

Okay, here we go. I just move this box, and there – see the handle? It's actually a door. Mind, these stairs are old and narrow. Watch out for the tight turn at the top, here. There we go. Welcome to the office!

And here's where I keep the Auchentoshan... just the thing for an occasion like this. And a couple of tumblers, keep it proper. Go on, have a sip. It's good stuff. There you go...

About the Kelmscott... I did have it, you know. Can you guess where I had been keeping it all that time? Yes indeed, it was in this office. Turn around and you'll see my glass cabinet. I'd been keeping it in there. So, after I'd tidied up all the fallen books, I came up here to look at the book and consider what I should do.

I like to think that my books act as wardens, keeping out low-level sorts of trouble... You might conclude that was the reason why all the bookshops got left alone in the riots – which I've heard said – but no, books can indeed be prized material objects, and just as prone to pickpockets as cheese and fillet steak for those with the want but not the means. The rioters just had different material objects in mind. Books do get stolen. Believe it or not, the sort of book *you're* after tends to be stolen the most. As if these would-be magicians think a stolen book on how to do magic is somehow more imbued with magical energy – or deviant energy, perhaps. However, the other sort of book that gets stolen a lot is a rare book, like the Kelmscott I held in my hands that day; the one I had lied about having in my possession. It should have been quite safe in this little annexe – a very determined ne'er-do-well could find it out, I suppose – but at that time I felt utterly convinced otherwise, and I can't explain why.

The Kelmscott was in the glass case you see behind you, huddled for company against another book made of vellum, Oliver Goldsmith's *The Vicar of Wakefield,* and a copy of Marquis de Sade's *Justine*, bound in distinctive light tan leather. These three were perhaps the most valuable and rare books in the entire shop. I assumed that the rude woman I'd thrown out, seemingly cold to ordinary books for the treasure of words within, was interested solely in their monetary value, and all three were at risk if left in the office, so I took them home with me that night. Which turned out to be a very silly idea…

Ah, I can see in the glass cabinet now is one of the books I was going to show you. Here, let me just reach past you. There. That's a 1960s facsimile reprint of *The Ancient Science of Magic* translated into English from the original sixteenth-century German in the 1800s. Contains a rather good ritual for making a magical sword. If that's the sort of thing you're after, I can do you that for eighty quid. Very good price. No cheques, I'm afraid.

However, I rather suspect you might be after something a little more… exceptional. Something extraordinary. Yes?

I might just have the sort of thing you need, but I must caution you. So many souls walk through my door in search of a little *magic*: teenage girls with broken hearts; cuckolds seeking vengeance on their rivals; victims seeking restoration from the universe. Twee little books of love charms are ten a penny, of course. Delia Smith-like cookbooks of the occult, which include recipes for cocktails that taste unpleasant, but offer no change in the practitioner's actual circumstances. That sort of thing is always turning up in stock. But the sorts of things I can procure for you aren't for the likes of just *anybody*.

Lots of books are special, of course. Like that little Kelmscott: a simple tale concerning a trickster fox, but oh so very fine and precious.

I took the book home that night – and the other two I'd picked up with it – driving with them on the seat beside me; the full moon ever at my back. When I got home, I went into my kitchen, set a pot of coffee on the go, and pulled up a chair by my breakfast table where I had put down the books. I picked up the Kelmscott and read the pages by the light of the single bare bulb – I don't believe in lighting up the whole house for no reason – speaking the words aloud as I read, all the better to comprehend them:

"Now go forth Grymbart and see wel to fore yow, Reynart is so felle and fals and so subtyl, that ye nede wel to loke aboute yow, and to beware of hym."

And so on and so forth...

As I read the words, I heard a sudden shuffling noise. It made me stop for a moment and look around the floor, wondering if it had been a mouse I had heard. But I couldn't see anything. All I could hear was the drip and gurgle of the coffee machine. Then I heard the shuffling again, quite close to my ear. I regarded the books on the table. *The Vicar* looked as dormant and dull as any school text. But there was something strange about the Marquis de Sade book. I looked closely at the cover, noticing with dismay a semi-circular slit in the surface that hadn't been there before. Had I damaged it on the journey home in the car? What could have caused it?

As I brushed the mark with my fingertips, the scar appeared to widen. A gelatinous line appeared; the colour of buttermilk. The leather peeled back, revealing what looked like a flattened eyeball, the iris as opaque as a dead shark's. The thing was apparently animated by a monstrous sentience, however, for it *looked* at me. Why I did not leap away in alarm, I cannot say. Instead I remained remarkably calm. I wondered if I were tired and rubbed my own eyes, feeling the barely yielding form of my own eyeballs behind my lids. I looked at the book again. Smiling to myself, I pointed my index finger towards the eye of the book in a poking gesture and watched as the lid clamped shut. I stroked the wrinkled leather and found it rough and firm to the touch. It was no eyelid at all. Just a fault in the leather. I laughed. I must have been seeing things!

I turned then to *The Vicar of Wakefield* and read the Advertisement, which goes something like:

"There are an hundred faults in this Thing, and an hundred things might be said to prove them beauties."

As I watched, something strange happened to the text. What I saw was now written in some sort of gobbledegook. I tried to work out the language, and realised that it was in fact still in English! But so horribly misspelled and twisted, it was almost an alien language visually. Reading the words, even to myself, was like hearing a bad foreign accent in my head.

"Ar ar a hundred felts in dis tin, and a hundred tinz mjt be sed tui pruv dem butiz."

It was as though the book *knew* my prejudices. Seeing those awkward letters filled me with a shuddering sense of horror and I quickly pushed the cover back down, lest the text transmogrify once more into something even more abhorrent – like text speak.

I turned back to the Kelmscott... only to see the words slide from Middle English to Middle Dutch to French and back. As the words translated and re-translated themselves, the sentences made less and less sense. I rubbed my eyes again. Below me the Middle English had re-asserted itself, and I read about the fox, dressed in his priest's habit, encountering two sister hens, Justine and Juliette. I knew the story well, and though the fox was suspected of murdering the chicken's daughter, the name of the child was Coppen. Something in the story had been corrupted.

I thought I had better pour myself that coffee. I took a long sip, and savoured the bitter, rich flavour.

Just then I heard an almighty *crash*. The sound of shattering glass. I glanced up. The sound had seemed to come from upstairs.

Very slowly and quietly, I pushed back my chair and padded out into the dim hallway. I keep one or two putters in the ceramic umbrella stand near the front door, for a little golf practice on the front lawn, you understand. I thought I'd best take one with me as I went to investigate.

I trod softly up the dark stairs, listening out for the creaking steps of intruders. I heard nothing. A window on the landing was letting in a little streetlight from outside; all else was shadow. Rounding the top of the stairs, I almost started at the movement of a ghostly apparition in the corner of my eye but, turning, saw that it was no more than my white summer drapes, billowing into my bedroom. A shaft of moonlight on the floor revealed the large lump of brick that had put the hole in the window.

Crash! Another noise, this time coming from downstairs. I had been duped!

Down I raced, back towards the kitchen, as quickly as I could. A figure in black was fleeing the scene; the books were gone. From somewhere inside emerged a spirit of strength and ire, and in rage I threw my putter at the thief's back. Of course, in the kitchen there were all manner of obstacles to get in the way of that missile, and the awkward shape of the object hammering through the air should have had it crashing cacophonously to the tiles. But had I been

Thor himself my aim could not have been more true, my strike more effective. The titanium blade landed messily on the back of the escapee's head. It was neither the heaviest nor the sharpest of the clubs I could have selected; nonetheless it cracked against the thief's skull and drew blood as it knocked her down – for the intruder was none other than the woman who I'd thrown out of my shop earlier.

I thought I had best make her comfortable, but first things first: I emptied the books from her holdall back onto the table. She was lying on my kitchen floor, which I am afraid was not terribly clean. I was just starting to think that perhaps I should call an ambulance, when she began moaning and came to.

"Hello," I said. "The police are on their way."

It was of course a lie. Her eyes widened. I thought my mentioning of the police had made her nervous. But her eyes were focussed at a point beyond my shoulder.

"Get. My . Book. Away. From. That. Thing," she rasped. I heard a rustling and looked up. The de Sade was leaning over the edge of the table, as though there were someone holding it at an angle; the eye glared down at us. The woman pushed against me and tried to get up. I found myself fighting against her, forcing her down, my full weight on her shoulders. She rocked and arched her spine to shake me off, took a side kick at my ankles. I lost my balance and toppled, and she got to her feet, taking another kick at my head. I grabbed her ankle and she fell back herself, slamming her shoulder against the corner of the fridge. I found myself grabbing a pair of scissors from the tidy, pointing the blades down at her. She grabbed my abandoned putter and – blocked by the cooker – took a weak swing at my shins, hitting the shaft against the table leg. I stabbed at her hands with the scissors, leaving angry red welts on her skin. I kept the scissors closed at first, but when I saw I was not breaking her skin, I went at her with the blades open.

She screamed, but managed to grab me by the wrist. Then it was her strength against mine as I bore down on her. I almost had the blades to her neck; could see the pulse in her veins there. I fought until one of the tips was near to slicing a mole in the V-shaped bone between neck and décolletage. We were both shaking with the effort.

"Stop, stop," she pleaded. "It's the book. It's making you do this."

"You broke into my house," I bit back. "I'm defending my property."

"Don't be an idiot!" she cried. "Can't you sense the build-up of energy in here? My book is a trickster fox. A *grimoire*. Read him one way and he's a villain. Another, a hero. In the wrong company he's easily corrupted, and can corrupt others in his turn. And not only do you not give him back to me, you go and put him with another of his kind. The worst of all! That book is *mad*. Debased and debauched. In other words – put that de Sade in your library and within an hour, your Enid Blyton books could all read like Irvine Welsh!"

I sat back on my heels, relieving the intruder of my weight – and the threat of scissor blades. "That doesn't sound terribly… evil."

The woman sat up and swished the hair from her face, releasing a long-held breath. "Don't be ridiculous. A grimoire is a magical book. Books are not moral or immoral objects in themselves. It's all about intent. The writer intends them to be read one way; the reader intends to read them another. The stronger determinant wins." She nodded at the baleful eye of the book, turned in my direction. "And then you have the determinism of the bookbinder."

She reached and with her uninjured hand picked up the de Sade. The book blinked at her like a curious child. "I've heard of a few examples of this sort. Anthropomorphic bibliopegy."

"Anthropodermic bibliopegy," I corrected her. "Yes,

I'd guessed it was bound in human skin. A lot of de Sade's early fans did this when criminal cadavers were more generally available. A lot of the covers had nipples, you know—"

"No, I was right the first time. Anthropomorphic bibliopegy," she interrupted. "It's my own term. It means the maker has ascribed human attributes to books like these. They are little characters. Rather simple ones, though."

"You're saying the de Sade is a corrupting influence?" I said.

"Exactly," she said. "And I would rather my little fox was returned to me, where he can be safe. There will be far too many creatures to sway his intentions at your shop. And he's good company for me." And then she smiled, all sweetness and charm, and I – I smiled back...

Oh – let me just top up your Auchentoshan. It's really rather good isn't it? So, yes, my little thief and I came to an *arrangement*. She was utterly forgiving of the wounds I had caused her. So very, very grateful to me she was. And so pretty. It was a shame to do her harm. She told me her name was Juliette, and whether that was her real name or not, it matters little.

Anyway, once I'd cleaned up the mess and blood I did a little research online about anthropodermic bibliopegy, and I hadn't realised it was such a lucrative business. One of those areas of bookselling where demand far outweighs supply – and the money offered! I tell you it makes the fine print and rare editions business look like spare change. A seller's market, if you will. Of anthropomorphic bibliopegy there was not a single hit, but of people asking for *grimoires*. Well, the world is full of saps. Nerdy characters for the most part. The victims of the world. Like you, Mr - . Ah, it doesn't matter what your name is. You are a victim, most assuredly. I don't know what your story was before you came to me. Perhaps you were bullied at school. Maybe your boss is mean to you. Perhaps you're crippled with impotence, or can't even attract a woman to your bed. It really doesn't matter.

You see, Juliette was right. The books are... I would say innocent, but that's the wrong word. They are *amoral*. Perhaps the writer wanted to spread certain concepts to the readers, perhaps the bookbinder and the bookseller had their intentions, but then the reader would need to be susceptible to all those ideas to be corruptible. And perhaps the reader can see beyond the intent of all those people put together. The reader can create something far more corrupt, far more insidious than anything the creator ever envisaged.

You look tired, sir. Let me take the glass from you now. It is almost time to conclude our business. I've kept you long enough.

You said you wanted to see a true grimoire – a book embodied with magical properties. Not a false conjurer's book of tricks, nor the ancient tome of a charlatan.

Here, I keep my most precious books in this miniature cabinet on my desk. The Kelmscott fox is the epitome of artistic endeavour and so I am afraid it is not for sale. I went to such trouble to keep hold of it; I could not even bear to let it go to the University collection in the end. Don't worry, they've had plenty more off me since. All sorts of unusual stock seems to be turning up these days. From the Kelmscott fox, I have acquired all my cunning.

Here is de Sade's *Justine*. See how she looks at you. From this creature, I have learned all there is to know about corruption and cruelty.

And look, here's her sister, *Juliette*. Just look at the work that went into that cover. I bound that one myself, you know. The leather I really wanted to use was too fine for the outer cover, but if you rub the paper on the inside you can still feel that little mole underneath. I also acquired my own press; it's in this building, concealed behind yet another door. An extra bonus chapter, if you like. I make all my own paper, and print on an old Victorian press. It's rather rustic, but works remarkably well. And of course, I've been bookbinding for years – quite a therapeutic little hobby. I love working in all the different materials. Especially leather.

And of course, last but not least, *The Vicar of Wakefield*. That turned out to be a grimoire as well. From him, I learned the value of a pleasant character and a trustworthy face. I do a very good job of seeming amiable. At least I like to think so. The lovely thing about grimoires is that they make the very best of people.

Now, sir, the time has come for my tale to end. And you, who came here looking for a exceptionally special grimoire are going to acquire the very best, and at no price to you whatsoever. No price but your soul. As I thought, the powder in your drink has taken effect and you are paralysed. I am wondering what to make of you. What adventures in your life would you have had with the courage of your conviction? A *Salome* I shall make of you, perhaps? A *Faust*... Then perhaps I will sell you to someone wise enough to not enter a secret stairway in a bookshop that sells such things as I do. Or perhaps you can stay here and keep me company. I always did prefer books to people. From one shelf to another, young man. Welcome to your new life. Now, are you sitting comfortably?

Good. Then I shall begin.

The Treehouse

Emma Coleman

"Can you hear me?"

No response. Silence, except for the dripping of the bath tap; I hadn't noticed it earlier but now, as I lay back in the tub, I allowed the sound to fill my ears. Drip after drip.

"Are you listening to me?"

The bathroom was crowded with shadows; some jerked across the walls as the candlelight twitched from a draft that crept in from the single-paned window. I was cold; the hot drops of water on my shoulders and breasts quickly became goose-pimples when the draft reached me. I didn't care.

I stared at my skin; I couldn't decide if it was pretty or grotesque; the tiny pinprick pimples made it seem as though I was being pulled by thousands of invisible threads. Being pulled towards the darkness.

The dripping of the tap roused me from contemplating the ease of disappearing into the black. The water falling around my immersed feet sounded like someone playing the spoons; a funny, cheerful little tune and, for a while, I was lost. I closed my sore eyes and was conscious of my fears slipping away.

The musical drip, drip, drip became urgent, almost as though the unseen player wanted to wake me from my peace, wanted me to feel my habitual anxiety. I was on edge. I was nervous and afraid, always waiting for a tragedy, expecting the worst.

I opened my eyes slowly, not really wanting to see that I was still on my own, still in my large dirty bathroom and still alive.

My skin was grotesque, I decided.

Movement on the far wall caught my attention; the

shadow spreading like the fingers of an open hand.

I sat up straight, the deep water rushing over and under my body. The player stopped playing, his spoons broken, and the dripping tap was just a dripping tap once more. The erratic splashes were loud in my head; I was confused, as if shaken out of a deep dream.

The shadow was shifting; the light of many candles bending, wavering and then settling, burning a beautiful orange, like almond-shaped apricots. I surprised myself by seeing something so lovely. And then I saw the cat. A huge, black and perfect cat on the wall. He was sitting in profile as though watching something intently.

"Is it me you're watching?" I asked of the shadow.

A strong breeze threw the flames out of calmness and the cat flickered out of shape. He soon came back.

I looked at myself and felt nothing. I may as well have not been there but the water was pretty in that light and I attempted a smile. Pastel hues of pink and green.

"So what have you seen, Cat?" I asked, while staring at my hands underwater. They were ugly and old. I looked to the shadow. His back was bristling. I turned my head to the left wall, to see what the cat had seen.

Shadows blurred separately and I could see a flock of birds; a dense, distant flock of birds.

"Are they starlings?" I asked the cat, "I don't suppose you care what kind of bird they are." And I slid back down into the tub.

Water ripples erupted and, like so many things, they slowed down and eventually disappeared.

My mind was full of birds.

"No," I said quietly, "not starlings. Nor doves nor swallows nor seagulls. Crows. I like crows."

I looked back to the flock on the wall.

"A murder," I said, "that's what I see, Cat, a murder of crows. Do you see what I see?" The cat didn't move. "Maybe you see mice."

Another cold breath from the window teased the candlelight and I watched the crows grow thin tails and long whiskers; they scampered across the wall.

"I see them too." And I shivered; the water was getting chilly and the draft felt wintry but I had no desire to move. Everything was insignificant, in thought and feeling, and I was detached from reality – I was in the cracked, cream bath tub in my old, cavernous bathroom and yet… I wasn't.

Three flames went out; the candles closest to the window extinguished like lives – poof, gone – and the room became a tiny bit gloomier. All that remained of those almond-shaped apricots was their souls climbing upwards and getting lost in the dark.

The cat was still watching the far wall; mice no longer played there nor did crows fly. It was empty; a great smudged, peach canvas tainted with the black cracks that crept up and across.

Another flame went out.

"Is that you?" I asked, softly. There was a high-pitched whistling of wind then silence. "If it is you, I'm going to tell you something. I'm sure you already know – you always knew everything – but I have to say this out loud; I'm tired of saying these things to myself, in my head. I'm scared, Mum. I'm scared of being without you. Things are festering in my heart and manifesting into beings of their own and I can feel them inside, all gnawing at me. It's only when I'm here thinking of you that I can push them down, push them away… well, for a while."

One more flame was lost, leaving only three candles around my bathroom floor and one on the low cabinet next to me. I looked again for the cat; he wasn't really there anymore, he was just a strange shape of pale charcoal, bits sprouting and spreading out of him.

"I don't feel as though there's much of me left," I said quietly, closing my eyes. "These things inside won't leave me alone and keep biting, ripping me apart. I don't want to be here anymore, I want to be where you are."

An unreal flood of cold wrapped over my shoulders and I flicked open my eyes.

One candle was alight; my heart beat a little faster.

"It is you, isn't it?" I whispered. My teeth chattered from the iciness of the room and the water temperature plummeted.

The flame flickered and grew stronger. The small bud was getting bigger and bigger, glowing a brighter orange. I slipped further down into the icy water, my chin now submerged, and yet I was transfixed by the light which twitched then briefly went out. As quickly as the light vanished, it returned with a faint crackle.

I was mesmerised, my vision beginning to blur; the fire was too intense, too consuming.

A black dot persisted in my sight so I shut my eyes. The inky circle was there too. When I opened them, the small, dark patch was behind the flame on the far wall and growing.

I tore my gaze away and desperately searched for the cat but I knew I was alone.

"It's not you, is it?" I whispered into the water, "Who are you?"

The menacing circle spread itself like a melancholy halo around the flame, overpowering the glow.

I watched as the round shadow became square, lines forming so quickly I couldn't believe what was happening, and this jet square was growing all the time. Now the size of a television screen, now bigger, now stretching, getting longer, and then the candle was blown out.

For a minute I was immersed in the pitch black. I dared not move and my eyes groped the void.

"What is *this*?" I cried as molten lava highlighted the lines of the rectangle, edges burning visibly, showing me a door. There was the sound of the wind whistling once more and then quiet. The lava became pale and all that remained was the perfect form of a door, as though a light had been left on beyond.

"What is this," I repeated flatly, hushed by the magic, but nothing else happened. All was silent; even the tap had ceased to drip and I waited in the cold water for something else, something frightening, but something never came.

"Is it you, Mum?" I sat up, the freezing drops on my body feeling like injections into my skin. "What do you want me to do?" I trembled. "Are you there, behind that door? Because if you are…" I tailed off, the sobs catching in my throat, "because if you are there, I'll come to you."

My shivering became uncontrollable; I wanted a sign from her, I wanted her to make my mind up for me.

"Please, I can't do this alone."

The candles re-ignited with a roar and lit up the dirty bathroom with white light.

"Please, Mum, if you're there then let me know it's you! I don't know what the point is any more; I've driven myself crazy with worry and hate and regret and all I want is you. You were the only one who knew me and now there's no one! I don't want to cope with the sadness and fear. I want everything to be as it was before you went from me or else for everything to just go away." I was crying freely; hot tears smothered my burning cheeks and my tired eyes blazed with truth. "Make everything go away!"

The candles were extinguished. The door on the wall flew open. The scent of lilac and summer evenings rushed through my bathroom on a warm breeze. My tears stopped falling; in that moment, everything changed.

"I can hear music," I whispered, as the voices of flute and guitars drifted towards me. As if the song had heard my words, the music got louder.

I was delirious from the intoxicating smell of lilacs and nightstock; wrapped up in a nostalgic haze, I found happiness pouring into me. I didn't care what was happening; all I knew was that feeling of utter abandon, the child-like joy and a wish for this to never end.

The music was enticing so I stood up slowly in my cracked, cream bath tub.

"There's nothing here for you any more."

I wanted to go through that door and, as I stepped out of the water, I laughed with a sense of freedom. The delicate breeze rippled over my skin and I boldly walked to this new world.

As I got nearer I felt lighter – as though bubbles filled my veins – and I floated through the open doorway.

My feet touched land and I saw earth between my toes. When I lifted my gaze, I was awestruck. A gloriously huge harvest moon was suspended above me against a wash of mauve and pink sky and yet I could see the outlines of a curved ceiling. A meadow stretched ahead of me; long sweet grass and poppies bobbed in the wind as if saying 'hello' but on either side were murals of great chestnut and apple trees, their leaves lifeless and flat.

"I love this place," I said softly, my hands reaching out to stroke the ears of swaying corn.

With my heart full of hope, I took my first steps into the meadow, giggling as I felt stems and petals brush against my naked legs.

I turned to look back through the doorway but I could see nothing, only darkness.

"There's nothing there for you any more."

The sound of the flute and guitars stirred me and I faced the horizon.

"I want to find the musicians!" I shouted gaily to the moon, "And I think I shall go this way."

I was blessed as I walked. Shrouded in a pretty, glimmering mist I was back to my childhood, reading tales of fantasy and superstition. I was a fairy. I was a magical being full of love. I sang to myself, creating the love I had for the music which was getting louder and clearer with each step I took. But still the dusky peach glow of the meadow went on.

"Where could they be?" I sang.

A great groaning creak made me turn to the wall; a horse chestnut tree had come alive, spreading its great canopy right over me. Sitting in a circle by the mighty trunk were the musicians, playing merrily. They were dressed like animals; a pig, a donkey, an otter and a toad.

"I know that you're a toad and not a frog because toads were my favourite when I was a little girl." I said.

They continued to play as if I wasn't there, so I began to dance; I was free and moved with sheer abandon. I was a graceful ballerina in a flowering rose tutu. The flute acted like strings tied to my body, every note gently pulling another exquisite line and curve, but the strong scent of lilac was intoxicating and I wanted it more than anything.

"I want to see the lilac tree!" I shouted.

The musicians played faster and I was spinning in a rainbow.

"I love this world!" I sang out, as streaks of colour whizzed over and around me and my rose tutu unravelled, revealing my naked body once more.

Eventually, everything slowed down and I came to a gentle stop in front of a cloud of purple. In my hands were sprigs of lilac and I pressed them to my nose, inhaling deeply. Oh that rush of innocence! That happy smell of the promise of summer!

The lilac tree was hanging heavy with dunce hats of tiny, purple petals.

"You remind me of the tree in my garden," I said, putting my arms around the slender trunk. I kissed the bark. "I used to do that when I was a small girl." And I kissed the bark again. I didn't want to let go but the breeze blew harder and the lilac tree drifted away from my open arms.

"Where are you going?" I cried.

"It's time for the picnic. The lilac tree plays no part in that."

A beautiful child wearing a golden dress took hold of my hand. She had a crown of daises in her hair and apple blossom began falling from the open sky.

"A picnic!" I exclaimed, "That's perfect! Will the musicians be joining us?"

"Of course, we can't have a picnic without music." And the pig, the donkey, the otter and toad formed a line and led us through the meadow, playing a lively tune.

Swarms of butterflies, beaming with scarlet and turquoise wings, flocked around us.

"We only have butterflies in this world, no moths," the little girl explained.

"Magical," I whispered, "And they always fly at night?"

"Yes, it's always a summer's evening here. An endless night of quiet beauty. Do you like this world?" she asked, turning her shy, grey eyes up to me.

"Yes! It's the world I've always dreamed of! When I was your age I used to pretend that I lived in a meadow like this and all my friends were animals and fairies. I remember being happy when I was a child… and now look where I am!"

I was giddy; the great, friendly moon seemed to take up the entirety of the sky and he was so happy to see us!

The ethereal insects flapped and fell around me; some even settled on my naked skin, creating patches of jewelled silk hiding my breasts and pubic mound, like underwear.

We continued to walk. Groans and creaks echoed around us as more murals of trees sprang to life.

"I've never known anywhere else," the little girl said, taking hold of my hand.

"You're very lucky. The world I come from has a lot of pain and sadness. It is beautiful but not to me, not any more."

She squeezed my fingers affectionately.

"You don't have to go back if you don't want to."

I looked down at her shining hair and daisy crown; she

was everything I'd always wanted to be and I pressed her hand tenderly.

"I know," I said, "and I don't want to go back. There's nothing left for me anyway." She skipped along by my side, her huge smile beaming across the landscape; everything was happy.

"A picnic then," I said.

"Yes, a picnic!"

"A picnic is one of my favourite things."

"I know, silly! That's why I got it all ready."

The next step I took brought me onto a red and white gingham blanket. Old fashioned glass bottles poked out from ice buckets, mounds of tomatoes glistened vibrantly and large chunks of delicious, soft bread were piled high.

"You did all this for me? But how did you know I was going to come?"

The troop of musicians stopped playing, put down their instruments and began to eat while the little girl sat cross-legged on the blanket and picked up a juicy tomato.

"Because the cat told me," she replied, biting into the radiant skin of the fruit. "He's your friend and he told me you've been wanting to come here for ages."

"A cat? But I don't know any cats," I said, sitting next to her and tucking my legs beneath me.

"You mean to say you've forgotten Jasper!" She gasped, her eyes wide with disbelief.

"Jasper!" And a thrill of joy shot through me.

"So you do remember!" She exclaimed happily and clicked her fingers; a fire crackle, a puff of yellow smoke and there he stood.

"Oh Jasper!" And I opened my arms out to him. He deftly sprang through the air and landed on me as I closed my arms around him. "You feel just the same," I whispered, playing with his thick, black fur.

"He's been waiting very patiently for you. He sits in his treehouse keeping watch and he saw you coming." She popped another tomato into her mouth.

"So are you joining us for the picnic, Jasper?" I asked.

He jumped from my grasp and prowled about the blanket.

"He likes sardines and turns his nose up at anything else," said the girl as she fumbled in the picnic basket. "Don't you?" And she eventually placed an open tin of silvery skinned fish in front of Jasper. He poked his paw at the contents and clawed out a plump sardine. I sat next to him, helping myself to a chunk of cucumber. When the taste hit my tongue, I was overwhelmed by the purity and how utterly delicious it was, but that was all there was: taste. Refreshing and delicate and yet I *felt* nothing.

"Magic," the girl said, watching me.

"Yes," I said, smiling, "magic." And I took another portion of cucumber.

Soon the picnic ended. I must have fallen asleep; when I awoke I felt drowsy and only myself, Jasper and the girl remained.

"Where did the musicians go?" I yawned.

"They have a lullaby to prepare," she answered, packing away plates and bottles.

"What a pity, I would've liked to hear that. My mum used to sing me lullabies when I was your age, she would sing quietly until I was fast asleep. "

"She had a very sweet voice."

I was aware of a distant emotion but I couldn't express what I was thinking.

"Can't we go and see the musicians perform? I'd like to, wouldn't you?" I asked, folding up the blanket and handing it to the girl. She popped it into the basket and, with another click of her tiny fingers the picnic basket shrank to the size of a matchbox which she then put into a pocket of her dress.

"It isn't time for the lullaby," she said, grabbing hold of my hand. "Come on, we're going somewhere else first! And you, Jasper, you can lead the way."

He sat up straight and sniffed the air, his long whiskers twitching like antennae, and then he pounced forwards, slinking away ahead of us.

"Where is he taking us?" I asked as we walked back across the meadow.

"To his treehouse!"

"Really? Oh how exciting! But what shall I see from up there? Is it very high? Are there a lot of steps to the top?"

She giggled and tugged my arm.

"So many questions! Just be patient and you will see for yourself…but yes, it is *very* high!"

The meadow was tranquil. The breeze had dropped, all the wildflowers stood up proudly and the huge peach of a moon bathed us in his dreamy light while all around us the trees bowed down, as if we were their queens.

"Which tree are we going to?"

"That one there!" the little girl replied, pointing straight ahead. Jasper halted a few feet in front and turned to me, almost smiling.

"What sort of tree is it?" I whispered.

"I don't know but it's always been here."

Like Rapunzel's tower, the soaring trunk stretched high, the top disappearing from view. The masses of leaves – all different shapes and sizes – painted a dazzling kaleidoscope, a patchwork quilt made up of the brightest, happiest colours.

"What an illusion the tree makes," I gasped. "You'd think there was no ceiling and we could climb into space!"

"Jasper often does but it's a different sort of space. I don't really like it up there. Somehow I feel older and frightened; there are too many steps for me and when I get to the top, I want to come rushing back down again."

"But what's the view like?"

The girl's eyes were cast down while her ruby lips gave a weak smile.

71

"It's astonishing."

She must be afraid of heights, poor thing, I thought and crouched beside her, putting my arms around her shoulders. She did the same; her small, slight frame fitted into me as though we were the lost pieces of a two piece jigsaw.

"Don't worry," I said, standing upright and holding her hands, "I can go with Jasper. You wait here and I'll be back down soon."

There was a moment when only the girl appeared to freeze-frame and everything else was alive; I still held her tiny fingers when her face became dead, her essence vanished, but for such a brief time I couldn't be sure anything had happened.

"Yes, of course!" She cried. "Jasper will take you to the top, won't you boy? Go on then, lead her up and see what's going on."

The sleek fur bristled – each hair looked electrified – as he sprang forward in a charcoal cloud, his green eyes flashing like witches lightening. He stood on the first step of the narrow, winding staircase and flicked his tail.

"That means he wants you to follow him."

"I know," I said, "I remember." And I followed my cat up the stairs. He jumped nimbly but slowly, all the while checking I was near him.

I glanced down to see the shining, golden bud of the little girl's head as she waved me on.

"Don't look back!" she called, cupping her mouth with doll-like hands.

"I won't!" I laughed out. I was delirious with the power of not caring and how infinite life seemed to me.

Jasper flicked his tail once more and I hurried my climb; I knew I was getting closer and was desperate to see what lay ahead. What new magic would I see?

"Hey!" I said and Jasper stopped, turning to me. "Will you stay with me forever?" He closed his eyes while his black, leathery lips curled upwards and I sat next to him on the final step. I picked him up and rubbed his pyramid ears with my cheek.

"Good, I've missed you so much!" And he purred like a wildcat – deep, guttural and threatening – but I knew he loved me more than anyone else in the world. "I've seen you in my dreams," I whispered into his fur, "and Mum. They were the best dreams."

Jasper looked out to the sky beyond the vivid leaves; the wash of mauve and pink deepening to dark blue and I was eager to say it.

"Shall we see what it's like, then?"

He sprang from my lap and into the doorway of the tree-house. I tentatively followed; I was waiting for and expecting something so beautiful I could barely breathe.

The light was strangely familiar; candlelight, but there were no candles to be seen, yet the pale amber and dark gold had deep shadows. My heart beat a little faster.

"Jasper!" I called. "Where have you gone?" He emerged from the inkiness, his green eyes sparkling.

"This way," he said.

"Jasper! Since when have you been able to talk?" I cried in amazement. He looked over his back and then returned his jewel-like gaze to me.

"I can't," he said.

Almost instantly his soothing purr filled my ears and I forgot my astonishment. His tail twitched and puffed out like an onyx sprig of lilac.

He's scared of something, I thought and immediately felt cold.

"What is it, Jasper?" I asked, moving towards him.

"It's time to look," he purred, and he led me to the two windows on the far side of the tree-house.

"Where did they come from?" A new rush of magic surged through my body as the large, almond-shaped windows engulfed my view.

They were empty; a void on the other side.

"Is that space?" I said quietly to Jasper who sat beside me.

"Wait," he told me, "wait a while longer and then you will see."

I put my hand down to touch his ears; they were warm and I realised just how cold I had become. My fingers felt frozen.

"I'm cold, baby."

Jasper jumped into my arms and settled on me, his hot fur was a dream on my goose-pimpled skin. My teeth chattered. And then I heard faint music. Music which drifted up from the staircase, filling the room with a beautiful melody.

"The musicians!" I stuttered, "They're playing the lullaby!"

I closed my eyes and lost myself completely.

When I opened them, I was staring down on an unreal scene.

I was pressed against one window, the panoramic view overwhelming. It was night time. The flame from a single candle was wavering sporadically, highlighting something.

"What is that, Jasper?" I asked. He purred but said nothing.

My eyes strained to see what was below me. Water; water shining darkly in a bath.

"Jasper?" I whispered.

The candlelight jerked and shone brighter.

"Jasper, what is that?"

A long, glimmering leg was hanging out from the bath tub; the eerie light making it pretty, as if in a photograph from a magazine.

The water was broken by an island; the belly button like an erupted volcano as the seas around lapped over the beaches.

My hands were tingling with intense cold and I tried to hold onto Jasper but he fell away from me. The lullaby was hushed; my ears were numb inside. I looked down at myself; I was naked again, the butterflies crumbling to pastel dust on the tree-house floor.

I couldn't think. I held my body – my shivering, cold-wrecked body – and realised I was wet. Water was running in rivulets along my arms and belly, down my legs and leaving ever growing pools around my feet. They were like halos of blood, moving and oozing outwards.

"Jasper, what's happening?"

I turned but he had vanished; all that was left was the dark, empty room, the oppressive shadows getting closer and closer.

I looked back desperately to the scene outside. I was terrified, ravaged from fear.

"It's me." I whispered.

I tried to scream, banging the window with my wet palms, but nothing came. The shadows were over me, crawling up my legs and wrapping around my arms. My vision dimmed as they spread across my face. I watched the bathroom fade into grey and then I saw nothing at all.

'Mum…' My only thought as I felt myself slipping dreamily away into the darkness.

Red in Tooth and Claw

Paula Wakefield

Are you comfortable? Got everything you need? Good, then let's begin.

I can't remember exactly when I bought this place. It was after my agent had sold the film rights for my third novel. You know the movie was disastrous, all that soft focus... And the heroine! Dear God! They turned a minor character into the major character... Better for the box office; young blondes always sell, they said. What I thought, what I wanted didn't count. Too late I realised I'd sold out, through ignorance, naivety. Yes, of course my contracts are now iron clad. It was after this that I decided I'd write the screenplay for anything else that sold; otherwise, no go, no way. My books and stories are the same – from the typeface to the artists, (whatever the platform), I have the final say on everything. I'd rather forgo a few million than be misrepresented ever again. Do I care if I'm labelled a control freak? Do I look as if I care? Do I sound as if I care? It always makes me laugh. Ohhh. Excuse me. Mary, some water please. Thank you. Such a lamb. That's better.

Oh no, no, no, no, I've no qualms about selling rights. Money is important. It buys time and choice. Women need to know that. But it has to be your own money. Your choice – right or wrong.

Besides, sometimes you can achieve on the screen what you can't achieve on the page. And now I'm hoping to support other women artists through my new publishing company, giving them the same security and freedom I enjoy. . Who knows what the future might hold? Maybe I'll expand into other media platforms.

Will I appear in another movie? Hmmm... That's really a reference to the so-called unkindness of the camera I suppose... A very veiled, though not well disguised, reference to my age.

A long time ago someone dear to me explained that age isn't chronological. So true, but so few understand it. I hope that you will, if you don't already. Anyway, the camera isn't unkind. The camera is neutral, or as neutral as anything else, any unbiased observer... but I, like most people, won't say 'no' to the gentle kiss of good lighting! In my experience, the answer is, 'have no fear'. I mean, if you are truly yourself without fear, guilt, shame, or self- pity, then the camera will love you, lines and all. I feel I've become, in a sense, ageless.

Of course I'd only appear in something I'd written and if I wasn't directing then I would have to choose who was. You know, I reached a certain age – I mean an age when I became certain – where I knew that I had to take care of me because nobody else would. I carry on doing that. And nobody, and I mean nobody, will stop me.

Once upon a time I'd had those romantic dreams, the Prince, the happy-ever-after. The Prince – pah! But the happy ever after does exist, (not that mimsy, mamby-pamby pastel coloured crap), you just have to create it for yourself, write your own story, ending and all! And write it in saturated colour, Little One. Be bold. Be brave.

Yeah, yeah, I've had a bit of work done. Why not? You wear make-up, much more than I do, despite your youth. People dye their hair. What's the difference? None, logically. Even dear Jane Fonda worked that one out. I think one of the reasons I've been misrepresented for so long is that I don't fit a stereotype – refused every one that's been hurled at me. I can invent and reinvent myself without any help from the corporations and their homogenised homilies.

So much rubbish has been written about me, some of it vindictive, a lot of it trite, all of it lies. One thing age does bring is, I think, courage, more courage than one has in one's youth, or maybe it is a different type of courage. Courage in all its guises is something I've always had plenty of. I know lots of women my age and older, not all of them wealthy, and they too refuse to be boxed, labelled, contained or constrained. You've met a few of them: Delilah, Goldie, Joan, Penny... when they've visited here... the best Poker players I've sat around a table with. They love it too, the wildness of the place, the privacy. Together we can be more than ourselves. We are a monstrous regiment. Tough shit! Better than meek, malleable, manipulated, marginalised.

I've always had such fun here. I can relax. And this place is so great for thinking. It's where I do all my work now. Of course it's changed over the years, you must remember how it was – Mary, ah, the best assistant I ever had, (now don't pout, jealousy is a waste of time and energy, unless you're prepared to act on it, use it – wisely), Mary can probably dig out some old pictures, taken when I bought the place... Nothing but a little cottage then. That was before you were born. Yep, I've certainly changed it, even since you were last here. Rebuilt (beautiful stone, all quarried from my land), extended... This is my creation too. I enjoy comfort; a little luxury... Things are just how I want them, and the household runs like clockwork. The biggest problem? The pool needs more attention in the autumn, because of the leaves and branches. But I won't have the forest cleared from around the house and, anyway, even I can't control the weather! As you know, my staff are great. Diana is the best woods-woman, and Princess keeps the pool at perfect temperature, year round. They are well paid and I respect them, they respect me and are loyal. That's something worth remembering, darling. They will never betray me. They know better. They're wise too. Ha! Nobody survives in the wild wood of life without wisdom, a couple of true friends and the occasional helping hand from Lady Luck. Of course you need to be wise, savvy and sassy enough to recognise Luck when she shows up. And then invite her in, welcome her, make the most of her. I couldn't ask for more. And I've no need to. I earned this. And when Lady visited me, I recognised her, wrapped my arms around her and she has never deserted me.

Are you getting this? You're recording okay? Notes clear? Good.

This could be Luck visiting you. Hopefully you've found something you're good at and that you love. It's commendable that you're trying to carve out your own path. And take no notice if people say that by writing you're following in my footsteps, ignore any charges of nepotism. It is true that I haven't given an interview for ages, let alone an exclusive. But don't for a split second imagine that I am doing you some kind of favour. No one else could write our story except me and, after years of falsehoods, I've become one dimensional in the eyes of the world. I could write it myself but, for the same reasons, it would be seen as spin! I don't see you as a charity case. I am trusting you, and this is your chance to be brave, but remember what I've said – and whatever you produce doesn't go out without my say-so.

Now don't take this the wrong way, for Goddess' sake, but your mother didn't get this, just didn't get it at all, my choices. I suppose I was never the kind of mother she wanted. Busy with my career, though I never excluded her. And still she chose to punish me. Shut me out. But she chose her own life too, even after your father died. It's just very different from mine. Strange that we were both widowed young, both with a small daughter to bring up alone. It saddens me that she decided to martyr herself on her widowhood; poverty, false pride. I'd already had some success by then – nothing compared with now. I offered to help but she'd have none of it. She stayed away.

Ahhh... but at least she allowed you to visit. She must have helped you with that baking at first, when you were very young– the bread and those delicious little tarts – but she never came. She decided to stay off-stage, not even a minor character...

And you did enjoy your visits didn't you! And I always

made time for you, even though I'd no idea when you'd turn up. And month by month as the moon blossomed and wilted and blossomed again, so you visited, and grew.

Maybe you thought you were quite grown up when you came to that party here. I'd already started turning this place into something special. Lupo and I hadn't been together long and – ha! – he had a hand on some part of my anatomy all night long, which is just how I wanted it. We still feel the same way about each other. But that night you were blind to anything but some longing, some desire of your own and I could smell the jealousy on you. You wanted him.

You'd also dressed in red, a colour I favour. Were you trying to compete? Oh, it's of no consequence. You were too young for that colour. I feel it's a colour a woman has to earn. Maybe you're still not ready for it? Mmm? Maybe you'll never be ready for it? And I don't say this to be cruel, darling. The ability to wear that colour, to stand out, to be a woman of and in the world, is something only you can develop. Don't let others decide for you.

I think you'd had some champagne. Your mother would probably have been angry. I'm not even sure she knew you were there, with us. You'd brought a basket of biscuits and jam. Very sweet.

Anyway, the party was in full swing, Bruno was being boorish I remember, Scarlet – superb as always, Marilyn, magnificent. You sidled up to us, Lupo and me. You were chattering at him, flattering him, but though he tolerated you, laughed politely, you knew he wasn't the least bit interested in you. So, you turned your attention, and your pique, on me. Presumably you imagined that by being unkind about me, Lupo would notice that you might be closer to him in chronological age than I am. You wanted him to see you. And he saw you all right – simpering – and he heard your absurd childish cruelty.

"Oh, Grandma, what big eyes you've got. And your ears are big too! I swear I never noticed 'til this minute."

Lupo and I fell into each other, laughing.

"All the better to see and hear you with, my darling!" I was indulgent in my happiness.

"And Grandma, what a big nose you've got."

I got it. "All the better to sniff out your little game," I whispered to you.

But you couldn't stop yourself. "Oh, Grandma, what big teeth you've got!" You giggled, but you hadn't finished. "I hadn't realised you were so long in the tooth!"

You saw it, didn't you? What I'm capable of. You smelled it on my breath – my intention. "All the better to eat you with, my dear... should the need arise."

And Lupo roared with laughter, and kissed me. And I kissed him back. I kissed him until his lips bled and he licked them and his eyes sparked with desire for me. And you ran; you ran out of the house, this house, my home, which Lupo still shares with me. You ran, crying, back to your mother. Or did you? Did you run away? Or did you stay out there, amongst the trees until all my guests had gone and I took Lupo upstairs to my room? As I drew the curtains against the night I thought I saw you, hiding out there, the cold moon caressing your hair as you listened to Lupo and me tearing our way through the night and howling in lust at that same moon.

So there it is, at last, my story. Lupo and I still living happily out here in the woods. You're very quiet. Hmm... I feel there shouldn't be any misunderstandings between us, granddaughter, and I hope you see this as an opportunity to make a name for yourself. Your choice, your name. This is my gift to you. And now you can write my – our – story, or at least these parts of it. Put your own name to it. In it. Make your own mark.

Still nothing to say? Okay. Let's leave it there but... And remember this; make no mistake, my dear: one sentence, one word that misrepresents me, that fails to do me justice, and I will eat you alive.

The Private Ambulance

Simon Kurt Unsworth

Elise drove a private ambulance.

Unlike most ambulances, this one was dressed in a monotone, sombre grey, had no sirens or flashing lights, and the patients it carried were beyond treatment or help or hope of recovery. There was no need for rush, no pressure on Elise to arrive at her destination quickly, there was simply smooth movement of the world rolling past the windows and the knowledge that in the vehicle's chill rear, her passengers rode in silence. She never turned the radio on when she drove, despite the fact that the ambulance's cab was separate from the back section, feeling somehow that it would be disrespectful during these final journeys. Elise gave the dead serenity and grace wherever she could, quietness after life's noise.

These night-time rides were the ones that she enjoyed the most; there was little traffic, especially out here where the buildings had given way to farmland and the ground rose to hills, and she could drive without effort or concentration, letting her mind reach out into the sky and land around her and find shapes and scents and sounds that, she thought, few other people ever felt or smelled or heard. Old man Tunstall's funeral parlour was out in one of the villages, serving the isolated communities scattered throughout the farmlands. Actually, they maybe weren't isolated communities, Elise thought, but one huge community stretched thin and laid across the hills and valleys and fields like a net, hundreds of individual strands twisting around each other in links that stretched from farmhouse to terraced street to barn and back to farmhouse. Few people escaped the area, once arrived, not for any length of time; Tunstall had once told her that most of his business was what he called "in-house", people from the area dying at home and being buried in the land that had sustained them. It was only occasionally that Elise was called on to take a body from the hospital in the city to Tunstall's, and the runs were always at night.

Outside, the ground was dusted with frost and occasional banks of snow. It had been bitterly cold these last few weeks, the earth hardening, becoming frigid, and Elise drove slowly, letting the vehicle's weight give it grip on the iced surface. The roads glistened in the dying moonlight and, around her, the fields drowsed under a caul of ice and the journey was all that mattered, this last journey between the places of life and the places of death.

Elise carried only one traveller that night. "He killed himself," the morgue attendant had told her in a voice somewhere between glee and horrified awe, "and we don't know who he is!" The man had apparently walked to the banks of the river that wound down from the hills, passing through the town on its way to the sea, stripped, knelt down on the ridged and furled mud at the bitter water's edge and frozen to death. His clothes were in a bag next to Elsie now, neatly folded, the top of the bag rolled and held down with tape.

"He was frozen solid," the morgue attendant had said, "and we had to defrost him like a piece of chicken!" Elsie had met people like the attendant before, people for whom the mechanics of death were the most fascinating part of the journey, for whom the biology of things was the most important. There had been the paramedic who had told her, voice rich with undisguised fascination, about the suicide who had jumped from a tall building and landed on the ground at an odd angle. Their head, said the paramedic, had connected hard with a kerbstone and cracked open and their brain had burst free and slithered, almost intact, across the road "like a big pink snail"; he had asked her out for a drink after telling her this. She had refused, politely, and taken the suicide's body into her private ambulance to begin its next stage of the procession into the ground. For Elise, death wasn't a moment; rather, it was a string of moments, a set of markers that led from life to burial or cremation, to earth or fire, and she saw herself as a companion and guide to these, the most significant of journeys.

The rear of the ambulance shifted slightly as she went round a corner, the wheels slipping over ice, and she slowed.

The dead man was being delivered to Tunstall's Funeral Home simply because Tunstall had a council contract to deal with the unidentified dead; there were spaces in the graveyards out here. In the cities, space for the departed was rapidly being filled and the real estate of passing on carried heavy costs that council couldn't pay, so people like Elise's passenger were sent out, to where populations were lower and the grounds cheaper.

The rear of the vehicle shifted again. There was a noise as it shifted, a gentle knocking.

Elise slowed again, dropping smoothly through the gears, letting the engine quieten. There was another thud from behind her, and a slight shiver ran through the vehicle. Had she run over something in the road? A rock or branch, maybe an animal? She glanced in her wing mirror but the road behind her, painted in fragile moonlight, was clear. She let her speed creep back up, happy that all was well. Elise took the dead man on.

Another thud, another slight shiver. Movement. In the rear of the vehicle.

Elise's first thought was that something had come loose back there, one of the straps holding the man's coffin possibly, that it was flapping, but no; the thud had been too loud and the shiver too heavy to be caused by a simple loose strap. Perhaps the coffin itself was moving, slipping on its base and banging against the vehicle's wall when she went around corners?

Another corner, slower now, but no accompanying

shift or thud, the road straightening, letting the ambulance speed up and then a definite bang from the rear. Elsie started, the tyres shimmying across the surface of the frozen road before she grasped the wheel and brought the vehicle back into line. The bag of belongings next to her fell from the seat into the foot well with a rustle of plastic and sound that was almost organic, like an owl opening its wings and stretching. Making sure the road was straight ahead for a while, Elise turned and tried to peer in through the small observation window between the cab and the refrigerated rear section. The glass was dark, throwing back a reflection of her face, eyes inked pools below her pale forehead.

She turned back to the road, lifting her foot from the accelerator and taking the vehicle gently left, in towards the roadside. When it came to a halt, she put the ambulance in neutral and unclipped her seatbelt, turning properly to the observation slit. Cupping her hands around her eyes, she peered into the blackness that travelled at her back. It was almost absolute, a gloom that was broken only vaguely by pale edges and shapes.

Something moved loosely in the dark and then the engine of the ambulance abruptly cut out.

Elise jerked back from the glass. What had that been? She twisted back around and turned the key, starting the vehicle again. The engine sputtered for a moment, caught and slipped, caught again and grumbled to full life. She opened the driver's side door and stepped out, leaving it open so that the cab lights fell across the road. There were no other lights out here, no streetlamps, no cars or trucks barrelling along the road, just the stars above her and the moon dipping low as the night came to its end. She made her way to the rear of the ambulance, reached out and took hold of the handles, felt the cold bite of chill metal against her fingers and palms, felt rather than heard something bump behind the doors, and then swung them open.

Everything was in its place. The coffin and its

inhabitant were still on the lower ledge of on the right side, where she had placed them, and the straps around the wooden box were still tight and fastened. She climbed in, crouching and pulling on the padded nylon cables; there was no give in them. She looked around, seeing nothing that shouldn't be there, nothing loose that would have explained the movement or the sounds. Experimentally, she placed her hands on the end of the coffin and pushed, wondering if the noises had been caused by it moving up and down rather than swinging sideways, but the casket remained still. Something inside it, then? No, she had watched as the dead man had been placed inside, the padding arranged around him to prevent precisely the kind of movement she was wondering about.

There was nothing on the other ledges, three of them, that could have moved. The rear of Elise's ambulance was, as ever, neat and clean and a fitting cradle for the dead on these, the last of their courses.

The engine, then, or something mechanical underneath the vehicle. She would simply have to drive carefully and hope she made it to Tunstall's, then make a judgement there about whether it was safe to drive back. She returned to the front of the ambulance and climbed in, shivering in the warmth. With the door shut and the belt back across her chest and securely clipped she pulled away, keeping her speed low. The road was rising now, curling around one of the fells. It would fall and rise several more times before she reached Tunstall's, she knew, and wondered if the ambulance would make it. She dug her phone from her pocket and checked it; a good charge but not much signal.

Another curve in the road and this time something *definitely* moved in the rear of the ambulance, banging hard against the side and setting the vehicle rocking outwards on its axles before it fell back to stability, distorting the vehicle's balance for a moment. This time, the bang had been accompanied by a noise that might have been a sheet tearing or something flapping, a long low noise only just audible of the sound of the engine. Her foot jerked on the accelerator, sending the ambulance lurching forward and onto the other side of the road before she could bring herself and it back under control, return them to the right side of the centre line and to a better speed.

Before Elise could do anything else there was another bump, this time even harder, jolting the vehicle and making the wheel twitch in her hands, and long, drawn out noise like something dragging across metal from somewhere behind her. The dead man's bag of belongings slithered across the foot-well, the top pulling open and spilling the contents out. There were jeans and a dirty brown coat, pieces of paper covered in writing, and feathers. They must have been in the pockets of the jacket, dozens and dozens of them, *hundreds* of them, small and large, black and white and brown, speckled and plain, floating out in drifts. The smell of them, of the clothes, was rich and earthy, grimy with sweat and death and cold. One of the feathers settled on Elise's hand and she shook it off violently, not liking the greasy feel of it.

Another bang, another moment where the ambulance belonged not to Elise but to itself, another correction and control regained and still they were travelling on, Elise wanting to get to Tunstall's now, to get out of the ambulance and into light and company. Feathers drifted around the cab, dancing and spinning, as she pressed down on the accelerator, urging the vehicle to gather up the road and loose it out behind them, now sure that the problem wasn't the ambulance or its engine but whoever was in the ambulance's rear, *whatever* was in the ambulance's rear.

She risked a glimpse behind her. As she turned, there was a long cracking noise and the unmistakeable sound of wood splintering and something falling, the vibration of it rattling through the floor, heavy against her feet. There was a dash of pale movement in the slit, a pallid shape that rose behind the pane and then fell again, not a hand or a face but something indefinable, as though it was wrapped in linen or muslin.

The engine cut out as Elise jerked back from the glass, reaching out to turn the key even though she was still coasting forward, gears in neutral and nothing, nothing, no reaction from the ambulance except to slow and slow, inertia and the slope bringing it to a halt soon, too soon. The internal lights clicked off with a sound like a gunshot, the dashboard's glimmer suddenly extinguished. She put the handbrake on, ignoring the increasingly loud, repeating sound of flapping behind her, not looking at the glass, not looking at whatever might be peering through at her, turning the key again and again trying to start the vehicle. And then the thing with the head like a dog seated next to her turned and drew back lips from teeth that were huge and which were the colour of old, tarnished ivory. She shrieked and jerked back from it, fumbling for the handle and opening the door and falling out into the road a single frenzied jumble of flail and cry. Her shoulder struck the gritted concrete and an off-colour bolt of pain leapt through her upper body and she cried out again, helpless.

A series of taps and shudders ran through the vehicle, tiny vibrations that she could hardly see, visible only as a shiver against the distant night. Feathers, more feathers than she had ever seen before, more than could have possibly been in the bag, drifted out after her, curling and circling in thick clouds, floating upwards instead of down, rising on breezes Elise could not feel. There was another bang, this from the centre of the ambulance, as though something had struck the partition between the space of the dead and the space of the living, then the long drawn-out groan of something opening and the unmistakeable sound of coins falling into a dish or cup.

For a moment Elise had the terrible sense of having offended something vast and old and she screamed, a wordless apology wrenching out of her. In the now-dark cab of the ambulance, the dog-headed thing shook its head and grinned and held its arms out, and from all around her she heard the sound of beating wings.

Bite Marks

Jay Caselberg

When do you get your baby teeth? When does that first white shovel poke through your tender gums? Shovel, knife, axe, incisor, canine, it's all the same. They are teeth and teeth make the world go round, until you lose them. I need my teeth. I always have. As a small child, I was known as a biter. They called my parents in to preschool for a serious talk. We got past that. It was a phase apparently, one I would grow out of. I never did, I simply adapted. Lips on skin, teeth on flesh. They're not so different either. It is the pressure of desire, an act of love, though some do not believe that. They say that taste is really all about smell, but I don't believe that either. Each sensation lives in and of itself. We mustn't confuse them. I, for one, am never confused.

Me, call me Olivier. It's as good a name as any and a worthy reflection of the Europhile parents I was burdened with. I got over that, but then there were other things that I never wanted to get over. Never would.

The first real one was an accident. I'm sure it was. I never meant to break the skin. Perhaps I simply became a little overenthusiastic, but then, what's wrong with enthusiasm? Enthusiasm is an intimate thing too. Intimacy needs to be enthusiastic. Always. But then she started screaming, which broke that special moment. The other kids back then in preschool and later had screamed too, but at that age I was too young to know, to appreciate the depth, to understand the passion. What is life without passion, after all?

Before Jade, I'd had a few girlfriends and they were either into it or they weren't. None of them lasted very long. It didn't matter whether or not they experienced the feel of my teeth upon their flesh, pressing hard against their smooth, taut skin, there was something else missing. I didn't bite Stacey, but I came close. That came later, with Jade. The intimacy of penetration comes in so many different ways, but the teeth, the mouth, the lips; you cannot really get closer than that. At first, I tasted them in other ways. In the end, though, there is only one real way to taste. Jade was different. Dusky, dark, silky smooth skin, tight across her body, resilient. Jade. She was like a gem, a polished jewel. I had favourite spots, of course, learnt from experience over time, the inner thigh, the lower abdomen, the top of the breasts; these were the places that pleased me most. With Jade, it was one of our first nights together. I was there between her thighs, my teeth pressed hard against her silky smooth skin and then, the moment was too great, the rush upon me, and, caught up in that moment, the intensity, I bit.

"What the fuck!" she yelled and scrambled back on the bed.

"Oh, shit," I said, looking up at her. "Jade, I'm sorry." I could see the darkness of blood starting to pool within the teeth-shaped marks upon her thigh, the bruising already starting to form between those marks.

"What the fuck, Olivier," she said, her face gone hard.

I licked my lips, tasted her upon my tongue and knew then I needed more.

"Get the fuck out, you sick bastard." She held her hand up, her palm towards me. "Get out. Now!"

But I had the taste then.

I crawled along the bed towards her, eyes fixed on that slowly welling mark upon her leg. Just once I looked up and met her eyes.

"Olivier!" she screamed at me. "Just leave. Now!"

And then she started to scream for real and beat at me with her fists.

It didn't take me long to make her be quiet, my fingers pressed around her neck, and then to taste her more. By then, she was still, so still, incapable of enjoying the moment, unable to share it with me. For that, I still feel a certain disappointment. Nonetheless, we had our moment together and it was almost enough.

Jade was special, would always be special. She was my first. Of course, I remember each of them, every single one, but Jade was truly special.

You've seen the crime shows. She had become the victim. That's how they would paint it, of course. But no. She was my first true lover. I loved Jade deeply. I still do. I always will. Always. Forget their superficial definitions. Her taste is on my lips even now, the memory. I always tried to make up for that first time, but nothing has ever equalled it, that loss of my true, real virginity. Jade had given me that and, as much as I tried, nothing since has been quite the same.

The beauty of a large city is that there is so much anonymity. People move in their day to day, slave through their repetitive jobs, sucking up the boredom and then going home to empty apartments and a glass of wine, a solitary beer, a lonely television show. Nobody is connected to anyone else – not really. Relationships are fleeting, casual, and people move from one to another, discarding each like skins, desiccated and forgotten, the goodness sucked dry. I guess, in that respect, I'm probably much the same. My relationships are fleeting, but there's a difference. They burn like stars in the night sky, filled with passion, but by their very nature they are ephemeral; they cannot be anything else. Meanwhile, I scan the crowds, clamping my teeth together, grinding my molars and yearning. The touch of my tongue on the edge of my teeth reminds me but does little to fulfil. The thing is, the faceless population that defines a city is the perfect hunting ground. There is no retribution. There never has been.

There were others, of course: Fiona, Samantha, Sunita, Mary and more. All of them fleeting, all of them satisfying in their own way, but never enough. I was hungry. I was hungry again and when you are hungry, you seek out sustenance. It seemed that my hunger was becoming more frequent of late.

And then… And then, there she was.

I am not sure when I first became aware of her. She pinged into my consciousness like a missed phone call, one of those tell-tale indicators on your phone's display. You have a sudden awareness that something's passed you by and then, there it is, staring you in the face. Maybe I'd passed her on the street, stood near her in a coffee shop line, waiting to be served, and somehow, some way, deep within my cells, I had registered. Registered but not noticed. What is it they say? Looking without seeing? That's the way these things happen. I must have known for days, because there was a subtle tension dogging my waking moments, wound up inside. More than a week, at least.

Have you ever wondered what defines a victim? Oh sure, there's all sorts of chatter in the crime shows about Victimology, Profiling, but really it's more organic. There are those theories about how the propensity to become a victim is some sort of genetic marker, something buried deep within the chemical codes that make up a person's being. As if we could taste or smell on them something that triggers a certain response. Personally, I do not like the term 'victim.' It carries too much baggage. We can blame the crime shows for that, too: a superficial depiction of the real complexity of the relationship, the depth; because ultimately it's all about relationships, and I knew, knew without knowing her, that my relationship with Magda was something special or would be. Like destiny. Theories aside, at least it was chemistry.

Olivier and Magda. Magda and Olivier. Magda on her own. Just Magda. You see, that just isn't right.

When I finally registered Magda properly, it was in a supermarket. Mundane as anything, but you can't pick where these things are going to happen. She was standing in the fresh salad aisle, musing over an array of bagged lettuce and other red and greenery, an empty shopping basket draped over her left arm. I had almost bypassed the aisle entirely, but then, as luck would have it, I saw something at the other end. The section where she stood was about halfway along. She was peering down at the bag held in her right hand, looking as if she was inspecting the contents. I wondered then, what was there to inspect. Salad is salad. Somehow, she felt me watching and looked up to meet my eye. That brief moment of contact stopped me in my tracks. I felt it then – that rush. I took a deep breath and walked slowly down the aisle towards her, trying to pretend that every nerve end was not registering her presence at all. I concentrated on looking at the opposite shelves as if browsing. Already I could feel my teeth closing on that clean pale flesh, the subtle give, and then the almost breaking, the taste of salt upon my tongue. I'd start on her belly first. That was best. Her breasts on one side and legs on the other. Soft, pliant, that gentle elasticity; I could taste now. I closed my eyes as I passed her, took a deep, slow breath and walked casually past. I could feel my nostrils flare as I passed, supping the air, trying to capture the essence. I wanted to breathe her deep. My Magda. But then, I didn't yet know she was Magda, let alone *my* Magda.

I lingered at the automatic checkout, having grabbed a couple of meaningless items, and then I followed, at a discreet distance of course, dumping my purchases along the way.

Autumn was already upon us. The workday was closed by darkness, a damp wind and huddled bodies rushing past in bundled coats pulled tight. The smell of wet dust, the taste of the city swirled through streets made black slick with moisture. Wind stirred the electric, the sparks that course unseen around us, rubbing static against the senses. I was already on alert, and the gusting air only added to the tension. I watched her from my distance, safe and in shadow. She wore a simple but well-cut knee-length coat. Stockings, shiny black shoes that matched the dark hair and offset the whiteness of her legs. In one hand she held a plastic shopping bag. For an instant, she looked back behind her, but I don't think she saw me… At least, not then. I slipped back into a shadowed doorway, just in case, but there was no need.

After a while, she stopped at a bus stop. I melted back against a wall, waiting, still alert. I hadn't expected her to catch a bus. Workers hurried by, heading home, or out, but they barely registered. I was concerned then, because this was one of those bus stops that served multiple numbers. I had no idea which one she would take. The tube would have been easier. Before long, however, my patience was rewarded, because I could see the expectation. There was a bus nearing and everything about her stance told me that it was hers. As unobtrusively as I could, I neared the clustered commuters, merging with the line.

Having boarded, I passed her seat, letting my fingers linger on the seat back just behind her shoulders, biting my lip as I moved further back towards the rear of the bus, keeping her in view. The ride passed uneventfully, she alighted and I followed. I stood for an hour on the other side of the street from her place on a tree-lined avenue draped with shadow. I could feel her there, see faint shadows moving behind curtained windows. I knew which place was hers. Her lights had gone on shortly after she had disappeared behind the front door. Damp gusts blew wet leaves across my face, but I didn't care about that. The only thing that mattered was her, and now I knew exactly where she lived. It was enough. The taste of the city's night had been replaced by the taste of my expectation. I faded back into the darkness and, head down, made my way home, lost in the memory of her silhouette against the window shade. It would hold me for a few days, but not longer, I knew. If I could not find her in the city proper, I could find her there.

A couple of days later I found her in a coffee shop. She was sitting by one of those window seats, watching the passing parade. I saw her there and nearly stopped in my tracks. It took a couple of moments for me to regain the composure I needed, and then, as casually as I could, I slipped inside. The minutes it took for me to place and order and wait for it to be delivered at the end of the counter filled me with tension, but I was able to keep an eye on her from where I stood. Finally, the coffee arrived and, holding it in one hand, I made my way to the stool that sat beside her. She seemed not to notice me, her eyes fixed on the passing pedestrians, a large china mug cupped before her in both hands.

"Hi," I said and she turned to look. "Haven't I..."

"Seen you around," she finished for me.

I swallowed.

Gently, she placed her cup down before her and then reached out a hand.

"So, hi," she said. "I'm Magda."

There was a name after that, but I didn't really catch it, something Eastern European, Slavic, perhaps. Slowly, I unwrapped my fingers from my own cup, and reached to take her hand, my teeth catching the inside of my bottom lip, caught up in her gaze.

"And you are...?"

I remembered myself then. "Olivier. I'm Olivier.

She held my hand for just a little too long, her skin cool and smooth against mine, and I found myself with the urge to stammer.

"Well, good to put a name to that face," she said and smiled. "We finally meet."

Again, unconsciously, I was biting my lip. I looked at her, looked at that clear, direct gaze, and then at her shoulders, her arms. Despite the outside chill she was wearing a sleeveless top, but then I noticed the pale beige raincoat draped across the back of the chair.

"Do you work around here?" I asked.

"You could say that," she replied. "In a way, I suppose. What about you?"

"Well, I'm on a little bit of a break at the moment," I told her.

"Okay..."

"I had to come into town for something, and, well..."

There was more, but in the end it was only chatter. I barely noticed.

After a while, I started. "Listen do you want to..."

"Catch up for a drink later?" She had finished my sentence for me. "Sure. Let's do that."

We made the arrangements and then she stood.

"Until later, Olivier" she said and smiled. She placed her fingers lightly upon my shoulder, never breaking eye contact. There was something in that look, a promise that forced me to draw in my breath. She removed her hand from my shoulder and lightly brushed my cheek with the very tips of her fingers, lingering. And then, draping her coat around her shoulders and reaching for her bag, she was gone, leaving me staring out the window after her retreating form, my heart pounding.

Much later, we met, just as we'd agreed.

We talked, we drank, and then, as the evening wore on, our bodies grew closer together, our heads tilted nearer, and she reached in and kissed me, feather light, a flick of her tongue against my lips. I caught my breath, knowing then what was to come, but it came sooner that I had anticipated.

"Listen," she said, leaning back.

Around us, the noise of voices and people swelled and eddied, swirling around in the semi-darkness, and I was forced to lean in to hear what she was going to say.

She cupped a hand around the back of my head and drew my ear to her mouth.

"Why don't we get out of here?"

I pulled back and met her eyes.

I should have known then that it was all too easy, should have felt the alarm bells going off, but no; the anticipation was driving me now, the expectation and the visions already forming in my head.

"Can we go back to your place?" she said.

That never happened. That could never happen. Always it was their place, or the storage space I kept for one very specific purpose, never my home. It was too close. I hesitated, caution almost getting the better of me. I was usually so careful.

But Magda. There was something so special about this one.

We left. With barely a word passing between us, we flagged down a cab, touching, skin against skin. All I could think about was that skin. I dismissed the knowledge that the cab was risky, that it could be traced. I ignored the fact that my address would be known, my inner sanctum, the place where I lived. None of it registered, just her. There were things inside my home that I would not want her to see, but none of that mattered any more.

We staggered up my stairs with barely a thought and, as soon as we were inside, she drew me towards the bedroom; almost as if she knew exactly where it lay. That didn't register either. There were no words, just a deep animal groan from deep within her throat. She pushed me back on to the bed, crouched beside me, unbuttoned my shirt, slowly, fingertips lingering on the skin of my chest.

"Wait there," she said.

She opened my closet, found a tie, and then another one. Gently, and then more strongly, she bound my wrists above my head.

"Magda, wait, I...."

"Shhh," she said and then stood back, pulling her top above her head and then stepping out of her skirt.

My mouth was dry. Her skin was perfect.

Without further hesitation, she clambered up onto the

bed.

She lifted one leg across my body and straddled me, her weight resting on my abdomen.

"Magda," I said. "You are beautiful. You're gorgeous…. everything I have ever wanted." I drank in the smooth, unblemished expanse of her silky skin. I could feel myself panting, my tongue pressed against the hardness of my teeth.

"Shhh," she said and placed a finger against my lips and leaned back, running her fingers through her hair before looking back into my eyes.

"At long last," she whispered.

She grinned at me and her eyes went clear, white. In her mouth, behind the sharp tongue moistening her full lips, suddenly there seemed to be too many teeth. Suddenly, we were not alone. Others were in the room with us. I could sense them, could barely make out almost familiar shapes, but all I could really see was Magda.

"What's happening?" I breathed, shaking my head. For just a moment, I didn't understand.

"You know that, Olivier," she said. "I am here for you. I have always been here for you, waiting. You just didn't realise… not until now."

I looked into her eyes, those impossibly pale eyes, and I understood. Magda was not a victim. Magda could never be a victim. She was something else entirely.

And then came the teeth.

Oh God, they were sharp. Impossibly sharp.

There was to be retribution after all.

Inspiration Point

Marie O'Regan

Her first thought was that she was blind. She'd opened her eyes, she *knew* she had – yet all was dark, not so much as a chink of light anywhere. She stilled her breath and listened, but heard nothing. When she could hold her breath no longer she inhaled quickly – a great, whooping gasp – and was relieved to find that she could, at least, still hear.

Her hands were bound, and so were her feet. She could feel the ropes biting into her skin at wrist and ankle, blood welling around them – she must have been struggling, then. Try as she might, she couldn't remember how she'd got here, or who had done this to her. The floor was hard, damp, and things scrabbled about in the dark – perhaps she was in a cellar? She tried not to think about rats, but couldn't help it. The scrabbling came closer, and she flinched, relaxing only as it faded away again – but not completely. Checking herself for injuries she was relieved to realise that – apart from a throbbing at the back of her head – she seemed unharmed. She tried to sit up, and her head started to swim. Dimly, she was aware of everything fading, then it was gone.

"What's your name?"

"What?" Reality flooded back, and she realised she'd passed out. She tried to sit up, unsure of what she'd heard, if anything.

"I asked, 'what's your name?'." the voice said again. It was a girl, perhaps around her own age – she certainly didn't sound old; maybe nineteen, twenty. The sound came from her left, and, she thought, a little behind her. She twisted as much as she was able, but saw nothing – pain in her protesting skull the only reward for her trouble. She groaned, and relaxed back against the wall as much as she could.

"Marnie," she replied. "My name's Marnie." The answer surprised her; for a moment there she'd had no idea.

"Marnie what?"

Now that did fox her. She couldn't remember. Marnie's head throbbed, making her stomach roll, and for a moment she worried about exactly how hard she'd been hit. She tried to sit upright, and this time almost succeeded. There was a coppery smell she realised must be blood, and the thought it was her own made her nauseous again. Defeated, she slumped back against the wall.

"Can't you remember?"

Marnie shook her head, regretting the action even as she did so. Her stomach lurched; she took a deep breath to try and quell the nausea. What if she'd done something serious to it? What if no one rescued her and things just kept on getting worse? What if...?

The voice came again. "Well, I can't see you, but I'm guessing the lack of response means no."

Marnie sighed, brought back to earth by the intrusion. "I'm sorry," she said. "I mean no, you're right. My head hurts."

"Did you bang it?"

"*I* didn't," she said, "but someone else certainly did."

The voice oozed sympathy. "Oh, poor you. Are you bleeding?"

"I don't think so," Marnie replied. "Not any more, anyway."

There was silence for a while as Marnie tried to gather her thoughts. Her companion gave no sign of wanting to continue the conversation, which suited Marnie just fine.

The darkness was slightly less pervasive now, she thought. It was still dim, but she could see a lighter patch off to one side, presumably a window. Perhaps it was dawn?

Turning her head to the other side, she could see a line of light some distance above her. At a guess, she figured that to be where the cellar door was. She smiled to herself, pleased to have worked out that she was probably in a cellar. That was no practical help, but it made her feel a little better.

Something scraped on the floor above, then thumped, and Marnie tensed. The noise passed, and she dared to breathe once more – then remembered she was no longer alone. "What's your name?" she asked.

"Annie. Annie Bourne." The girl's tone was matter of fact, a slight tremble in her voice the only sign she might be scared.

"How did you get here, Annie?"

"I'm not sure. I remember sitting down on a bench at the bus stop… and then I woke up here."

Marnie thought about that. Her own last memory prior to this was of walking home, and a blinding pain at the back of her head. "You don't seem scared," she said.

"Oh, I am," Annie answered. Her voice got small. "I just . . . try to make the best of things, I suppose."

Marnie laughed. "Not sure how to make the best of something like this, but I admire the sentiment."

"Do you think we'll get out of this?" Annie's voice was less certain now; a quaver had crept in, revealing her lack of confidence.

Marnie cursed herself for undermining the girl; she was just trying to keep herself under control. "Of course we will," she answered; unwilling to deal with Annie if she was going to have a meltdown. They needed to stay calm, figure out what was going on.

The scraping over their heads sounded once more, and Marnie felt the other girl huddle in closer. She hadn't realised how close they were, or how tightly Annie must have been holding herself – so had she, come to that. The warmth of her companion's body was welcome, however slight, and Marnie felt the aches in her own body complaining at the unaccustomed increase in temperature, however slight. A floorboard creaked, sending a shower of dust down on to their heads, and Annie whimpered.

"Sshh," Marnie whispered, and the girl huddled even closer. For long moments they sat there, barely breathing, waiting for some sign they'd drawn the attention of their gaolers – nothing came.

Gradually, the two girls relaxed. Marnie could see more now – the lighter patch over to her left was indeed a window, covered with what looked like a piece of grubby sacking nailed roughly over the frame. With the increased visibility, Marnie realised she could now probably get at least an idea of what Annie looked like.

"Annie?"

The girl was silent, Marnie could sense no movement. Had she fallen asleep? She started to turn her head, moaning at the pain induced by this movement – both the wound at the back of her skull and the stiffness in her neck protesting at such treatment. She winced as something pricked her hand, and darkness fell.

"Marnie?"

The voice was shaky, struggling to maintain calm, and Marnie recognised it as Annie's. She flicked her tongue across her lips, attempting to soothe her cracked mouth, but it felt too large, somehow alien – dry and rough.

"*Marnie!*"

It was more insistent now, and Marnie realised some sort of response was required – but nothing came. Her wrists were agony, she'd slumped forward and the ropes were biting into the soft flesh there – so there wasn't just a wall behind her after all, was there. Or if it was just a wall, there was a ring or a hook or something that her ropes were fastened to. She forced herself upright, and gasped at how badly that hurt her. She tried to speak. "I..."

"Oh, thank God."

Annie had given up looking on the bright side, it seemed, and Marnie had to feel a twinge of sadness at that. She tried again, and this time was more successful. "I'm okay. I think."

She became aware of various pains she hadn't noticed before – her hand stung where something had scratched her before... before what? Her back ached, and her ribs felt bruised – there was a sharp pain when she tried to take a deep breath, so she struggled to keep her breathing light. Why wasn't that as easy now?

Annie was almost hysterical. "I thought you'd died! You went all quiet and then you sort of... drooped, and wouldn't answer me! I thought you'd had a stroke, or..."

"Annie!"

The girl stopped in mid-flow, her breath hitching as she tried to regain control. There was no trace now of the brightness she'd displayed at first.

Marnie tried to temper her tone, sorry she'd been sharp. "Calm down, okay? We need to figure out where we are, what's going on."

Annie muttered something incomprehensible that Marnie chose to take for assent, and she turned her attention to what little they knew of their predicament.

"Neither of us know how we got here, right?" she asked.

"No," Annie said.

"Are you hurt at all?"

"No," Annie answered.

Marnie pondered that one for a while. She'd been hit on the head, knocked out with what she suspected was an injection this time around, then apparently beaten whilst unconscious. At best. How had Annie not been touched?

She tried again. "Are you sure?"

There was a pause before Annie answered. "My wrists are a bit sore, but that's the rope, isn't it."

"Nothing else?"

"No," Annie said. "But you've been here longer than me, I think. And what if..." Her voice trailed off.

"If?" Marnie prompted.

"What if they're saving me for when they're finished with you?"

Marnie hadn't thought of that. She sat and listened to Annie as she started to cry softly, and couldn't think of a thing to say.

Time passed, and the silence held. Marnie was frozen, horrified at the thought that Annie might be right, and she was meant to be Marnie's replacement, ready for when she was all used up – and presumably dead.

Annie herself didn't seem to want to intrude, leaving Marnie to her thoughts – for now, at least. Marnie was grateful for that. She tried hard to remember the events that had led up to this incarceration, and could only remember walking home from a night out with the girls, then a sudden blow to the back of her head. Then the cellar. She thought about her injuries, tried to catalogue them. There was the bump that felt the size of a mountain on her head; her ribs ached in several places and she still couldn't breathe deeply without a sharp, stabbing pain in her side – probably a broken rib, which she could only hope wasn't digging into her lung. No coughing yet, so she guessed she was okay so far. Her back was sore, too – part of this was probably the prolonged period spent sitting on the hard floor (her tailbone was sending bolts of pain up her spine every time she tried to shift her weight a little), part of it was probably down to landing like a sack of coal when she'd been hit on the head.

She couldn't feel anything else, other than the ubiquitous pain in her wrists. She leaned back, and hissed as they complained at this renewed pressure.

"What's the matter?"

Annie sounded much more guarded now, and Marnie

wondered how much to tell her. "My wrists are sore, that's all," she said. "I daresay yours are, too."

Annie's reply was a non-committal "Mm," and Marnie wondered what was wrong. She tried to crane her neck to see her companion, but Annie had shifted to one side and Marnie got no more than a glimpse of dark hair at the level of her own shoulder before she lost sight of her companion.

Silence fell again. Annie didn't seem interested in talking, and Marnie was running recent days through her mind, looking for a reason for someone to do this. She let her thoughts roam to her boyfriend, Cal, and a smile teased the corners of her mouth. Three days ago they'd been at a party, dancing close, laughing and – as always, with them – talking. She couldn't even remember whose party it was, other than some friend of Cal's. She closed her eyes and pictured Cal as he'd been that night; happy, green eyes crinkling at the corners in the way she loved when he laughed. Dancing had never been a strong point for either of them, and she smiled as she remembered his emphatic apologies when he'd trodden on some girl's foot. Cute thing, small and dark, and dancing way too close to Cal for that not to happen.

She opened her eyes. Cute, small, dark. Something shifted at the back of her mind, something she couldn't quite fix. Annie moved, and Marnie tried not to flinch. Then wondered why.

She'd had no warning, this time, of darkness falling. One moment she'd been thinking about... what, exactly? It had started as a nice memory, she was sure of that, but then...

It was gone, no use trying to get the memory back now. Her head felt bruised, *her whole head*, as if someone had bounced it around, banging it off walls and floor whilst holding on by her ears, which now felt huge and very hot. Not possible, she knew, but the pain was impossible to ignore – or to explain.

"Annie?"

No answer.

"Annie? Are you there?"

Something shifted overhead, and Marnie froze. She listened, breath held for what seemed an eternity, as footsteps roamed over her head. Her chest was burning now with the effort of holding it all in, but still she couldn't bring herself to let out any air – what if she was heard? Then she couldn't wait any more, and let out a sob as everything escaped. She stiffened in terror, sure she'd bring someone down to investigate the noise.

Nothing. No one heard, or if they did they weren't about to come downstairs, and she was grateful for that. Still, she breathed now – short, shallow sips of air that she could let out with little or no discernible noise, even by her.

There was a sharp bang from overhead, making her jump, and then a scraping noise – and Marnie was ashamed to realise she'd wet herself. She sat there, the warm fluid spreading beneath her, and started to cry. Had she really sunk this low, after what couldn't really have been very long locked in a cellar?

Apparently she had. The scraping noise stopped, and Marnie heard a groan – a man's voice, she was sure, and strangely familiar. Muffled voices rose in what sounded like an argument, then there was another thud, and silence fell.

Marnie was starting to doubt her own sanity. Still no Annie, and the light – what little there was – had waxed and waned at least twice. Now she was in darkness again, and no one had been near her for ages. There hadn't been any further sounds from upstairs since she'd wet herself, and part of her was thankful.

Groaning, she shifted her weight and wondered how long it took for pressure sores to start. Her backside and tailbone ached like a bitch, and her head now felt too big – at least it didn't hurt anymore. The smell of stale urine wafted up as she moved, and she felt the shame of it all over again. This time intermixed with anger that she hadn't been allowed to relieve herself, had instead been kept chained like a rabid animal and neglected for God knows how long. Her stomach growled, and Marnie tried to calculate how much time had passed since her last meal – she'd gone from raging hunger pangs to an empty, pinched feeling in her stomach, so she'd guess quite a while. Annie was gone, and had been for some time – Marnie was beginning to think she'd imagined her in the first place, made up a companion to alleviate the loneliness a little.

Something creaked, off to her left, and Marnie whimpered.

"Annie?"

No answer, save for a badly stifled giggle, and Marnie's fear ramped up several notches.

Something thudded against the wall by her head, and she started to cry. Up until now, most of the indignities had been inflicted when she was asleep, or unconscious. Now she prayed that her attacker would knock her out again, showing at least a little mercy.

Something scraped along the floor, metal on concrete, close by – mercy seemed to have run out. Marnie yelped as something prodded her in the thigh, and again there was a giggle – whoever it was didn't bother to stifle it this time. High pitched and cruel, Marnie recognised the tone. "Annie. I should have known."

So she had been real, that much was true. But she hadn't been a prisoner at all. She'd been Marnie's tormentor all along, pretending to offer a sympathetic ear.

Someone cleared their throat, off to Marnie's right, then there was a click – and the cellar flooded with light. Marnie clamped her eyes shut, too late; her head throbbed with the impact on her sight after so long. She felt someone fumbling with her chains and heard a click; then footsteps, running up stairs, and a door opening.

Silence.

For long moments, Marnie didn't dare to move. Finally, she unscrewed her face and allowed her eyes to open a crack, then a little more, trying to lessen the pain this new and vivid light incurred.

She was in a cellar; she'd been right about that. The concrete floor was clean, more or less, bloodstains dotting the floor here and there. Looking up, she could see shelves lining one wall – boxes and paint tins, presumably the usual cellar detritus ranged along their length. Over to her right there was a flight of wooden stairs, a single light bulb swinging over them. Belatedly, she realised just how used to the dark she'd become, to be so blinded by what was, after all, fairly weak illumination. The stairs dimmed as the bulb swung back and brightened on its return. There was another click, and now she could see that the door at the top of the stairs was ajar; someone had turned on the light in the room behind it. She heard laughter, high and shrill, then silence fell once more.

Marnie waited, aware that she had to gauge her situation correctly here; any mistake could be her last. For a while she could sense (or maybe imagine) someone waiting just the other side of the door, ready to fall on her when she walked through.

Still she waited. After a while she remembered the fumbling at her wrists, and tried once more to raise her hands. She was so stiff she nearly didn't manage, but slowly her arms rose and she could rub her wrists, crying at the pain as blood flow was properly restored. She groaned again as she put her weight on her hands and attempted to push herself upright. Her first attempt failed, and she slumped back to the floor, demoralised and wary of trying again. Then her new position started to get painful, and she realised she had to.

"Nothing ventured, nothing gained, right?" she muttered to herself, and laughed at how alien her voice sounded. Cracked and thin, the result of dehydration and lack of use for what must surely be several days. Something small skittered away at the unaccustomed noise, but Marnie wasn't scared of that now. After the events of the last few days, a mouse – or even rat – was the least of her worries. She knelt, feeling her knees pop and her back protest, and put her hands to the floor. She paused, then, just for a moment – taking a last look around at her prison, making sure it was safe to stand. Then she pushed up with her hands and hauled herself to her feet. She swayed a little, and almost reached out to support herself on the shelves, but then the floor stopped moving and she started to feel steadier. Her heart was racing as if she'd run the 100 metres, just from the effort of standing up, and she wondered again how long it had been. Would she deteriorate so much, physically, in a matter of days? When her heartbeat started to settle down, she moved forward towards her next target: the stairs.

They were creaky, and she moved up them as quietly as she could – flinching at each groan and crack of the ageing wood. Finally, the door was within reach – and she found herself too scared to push it open. In her head, her attacker was standing on the other side, waiting for her to walk through the opening so he or she could attack, and push her all the way back down – happy to watch her crack her head on the concrete floor, maybe even bleed to death or fracture her skull.

"Don't be stupid," she told herself. "You've got this far." Thus cajoled, she reached forward and took hold of the doorknob, her hands quivering as she forced them to do what she wanted.

Marnie's brain refused to process the image in front of her. She was in a kitchen, that much she could understand, but the sight of Cal tied to a wooden chair in the centre of the room, bloodied and bruised, would not compute. She whimpered, and saw him twitch; some semblance of consciousness remained, then.

"Cal?"

His head lifted slightly, then slumped again. He had no strength to lift it.

Marnie looked at the floor around him, noting the blood that had pooled and dried, and dripped again. How long had he been here, no more than what – fifteen, twenty feet away? She could hear him huffing as he tried to breathe through his nose and failed, having to almost cough his breath out through his mouth before hissing more in.

No one else seemed to be here, but Marnie knew she couldn't trust that. She inched forward, hoping that Cal would look up, and that he'd know her. That he'd be able to stand, and that they could get out of here.

She tried again. "Cal?"

This time he managed to raise his head a little higher, and Marnie gasped as she saw the extent of the damage to his face. He tried to speak, but managed only to moan, and drool more blood on the floor.

His eyes were puffed shut, and navy blue. His nose was smeared across his face, and thick blood massed around his nostrils, bubbling when he tried to breathe. His mouth was worst, though. His lower jaw was hanging, but at entirely the wrong angle – hanging off to the left, tongue lolling down. That was swollen and bruised, almost purple, and blood was welling from a jagged cut down its side – the cut seemed to have come from the ragged remnant of one of his canine teeth. His teeth were broken, shards of enamel littering his shirt, gleaming white against the crimson stained cloth.

"Oh God, Cal," she said, and went to him – all thought of danger forgotten now. She went to the back of the chair and saw that plastic ties were sinking into the swollen, puffy flesh of his wrists – the flesh below them already blackening and distended. Looking around, she saw a knife on the worktop a few feet away and grabbed it, trying not to cut him as she worked the blade under the ties and cut through them.

He groaned, but left his arms hanging – she lifted them into his lap, started rubbing them to try and get the blood flowing again.

"Not so pretty now, is he?"

Marnie flinched, and whirled to face the sound. "Annie."

Annie giggled, delighted. "*Ta dah!* Bet you thought you were going mad, didn't you." It wasn't a question.

Marnie turned once more, positioning herself between Annie and Cal. Annie stood in the doorway to the kitchen, head cocked to one side as she watched Marnie; eager to see some sign that she'd broken her.

Marnie straightened, stood with her feet firmly planted hip-width apart, and stared right back. "I gave up on that a long time ago," she said.

Annie's smile faltered. "I'm sorry?"

"You will be." Marnie took a step forward, and was gratified to see Annie take a corresponding step back. "I've played the nice girl long enough, I think." She turned and looked at her boyfriend over her shoulder. "Don't you, Cal?"

She was rewarded by a grin from that broken mouth, which quickly dropped when Cal's gaze turned to Annie.

Marnie's mind was clear now. The fog of the last few days had lifted – Annie had drugged her, she could see that now. How dare the little bitch? The flash of memory she'd had earlier returned, of dancing with Cal while a small, dark-haired girl glowered at them – and this time she recognised the girl as Annie. She was a little disappointed that all this was just a jealous 'screw you' from some lovelorn kid but she had to admit Annie had potential.

As Marnie watched, Annie seemed to gather herself. After a nervous glance at Cal, presumably making sure he wasn't able to come to Marnie's aid, she said – in a voice far braver sounding than she looked – "You had no idea it was me."

"No," Marnie said. "I didn't." And now her smile was brilliant, making Annie flinch. "I have to admit you were a surprise."

"I don't know what you mean," the girl answered, and her voice wavered slightly. "You always seem to get what you want, and you're so bubbly and pretty. You're always so nice to everyone..." Now her gaze swept across Cal's ruined face again. "You're like a flame."

Marnie followed Annie's gaze. "And he's what, a moth?" She started to laugh. "You thought you'd teach me a lesson? Show me I can't always have what I want? That it doesn't pay to be *nice*?" She remembered the knife in her hand, and launched it at Annie, laughing all the more when the girl screeched in fright as the blade slammed into the doorframe not far from her head.

She ran towards Annie, who shrieked once more and fled down the hall. Gripping the knife by its handle and hauling it back out of the frame, she yelled after her: "Newsflash. I'm not that nice."

Marnie heard the scrape of chair legs on the tile floor behind her and turned, happy to see Cal staggering to his feet. His face was a mess, but he seemed essentially unharmed, if a little groggy. She moved back to him and stood on tiptoe, kissed his forehead. "Welcome back, lover. Want to play?"

He nodded, sending a spray of blood onto the floor, and grimaced. "Think I'll take the dentist's fees out of her flesh."

Marcie saw the pain speaking caused him, and could barely understand his words. She frowned. "Sounds fair to me," she said, and moved forward again. "Come on."

The upstairs appeared deserted. Marnie stood motionless in the hall alongside Cal, listening. She could hear the wind, and rain coming down hard, which suited her mood. This felt like the right time for end of the world weather. A floorboard creaked and she cocked her head – no random giving of wood, this. Annie. The sound came again, and Marnie realised it was coming from the second room on her left. Floorboards creaked again, followed by the sound of a door snicking shut, and Marnie smiled. She nodded towards the room, and motioned for Cal to follow her as she moved forward.

She eased the door open as slowly as she could, not wanting to alert Annie to her presence too soon. The room appeared empty; bare floorboards were covered by a thin film of dust which showed Annie's footprints clearly as they led towards a door on the other side of the room – an en suite bathroom, Marnie thought, or a fitted cupboard of some kind. Either way, Annie was trapped.

Cal moved past her and positioned himself to one side of the door so that, if she opened it, he'd be behind her and well placed to grab her and hold their quarry, ensuring that Marnie could go to work on her.

Marnie let out a slow breath. This was what she loved; not the pretence of normality that she had to maintain day by day so that no one would suspect; not the playing nice that ensured people liked and trusted her, and by extension Cal. No, what she loved was cornering the mouse and starting to play, seeing the fear on a victim's face as they realised both their miscalculation and the fact that their error was about to prove fatal.

A sob, quickly stifled, came from behind the door, and Marnie relaxed into her role. She strode forward and opened the door, revealing Annie cowering in a cupboard, tears etching a path in the dirt on her cheeks.

"I'm sorry!" she wailed. "I didn't know!"

"That's an excuse?" Marnie said. "Pretty poor one, if you ask me." She looked over her shoulder. "What do you think, love? Should we accept her apology?"

"Not much of an apology," Cal growled. "I don't think she means it."

Marnie reached in and hauled Annie out of the cupboard, dumping her on the floor in the centre of the room. Now that the drugs were out of her system she was more than a match for the smaller girl, and ready to take her revenge.

She knelt down in front of Annie, pulled her hair to force her to look up and into her eyes. "You ruined our game, Annie. We were playing nice, lining up the next one."

"The... next one?"

Marnie nodded. "That's right. It's been months since the last one, and we were starting to get bored."

"The last one?"

"What are you, a parrot?" This from Cal, who aimed a kick at Annie's behind, and laughed at the cry of pain that ensued.

"Not yet, Cal," Marnie said. She turned to Annie. "I'm sorry about him, he's a little... testy about the way you treated him." She thought back to the party. "I thought you liked him; you certainly seemed keen at the party."

"He didn't want me, though, did he," Annie said. "He only wanted you." She looked down at the floor and went on, "It's always the same. They never want me." She looked back up at Marnie, and her gaze was defiant. "Why should girls like you always get lucky? Just because you're confident, and nice, and..." She realised the error in her assumption and faltered.

"So you thought you'd ruin him for me, is that it?" Marnie asked. "Spoiler tactics?"

Annie nodded, her gaze once more firmly on the floor.

Marnie tapped the knife blade against her thigh, thoughtful. She and Cal had travelled a long way together, finding a mark wherever they went; playing nice, earning trust... then obliterating their victim before covering their tracks and disappearing again. This time felt different. Their intended victim had been an insipid little thing with a crush on Cal, and both Marnie and Cal had taken great pleasure in encouraging her affections. Annie, though... Annie had shown guts. Sick to death of being passed over in favour of the prettier, more vivacious girls, she'd shown some spunk and decided to take her revenge. You had to respect her work ethic, Marnie thought. Then again, she needed to be punished, and she was going to be so much more fun than their intended prey.

Leaning forward, she whispered into Annie's ear. "You know we have to make you pay, don't you?"

Annie nodded, her sobs coming more strongly now.

"I'll tell you what, though," Marnie continued. "You showed promise, down in the cellar. I'll make a deal. We can leave you alive; you can take this as a lesson, a starting point." She pulled the girl's head upright and stared into her saucered eyes. "Do you understand?"

The girl tried to nod, winced. "I... I think so, yes."

"And when we're finished," Marnie said, "we'll give you her name. She can be your first. You always remember your first time, after all."

Silence. The wind sighed in the eaves, and the three of them sat motionless as Annie thought about that.

She nodded, and Marnie grinned as she raised the knife, watched the light glint off the blade before she went to work on her almost willing victim with its point. It wasn't every day you got to inspire someone.

A Boardinghouse Heart

Paul Graham Raven

Three days of room and board. Expensive, too close to the city. Slam door on innkeeper's boy, hands shaking. Mildew; shafts of sunset sneak through shutters. Joints burn bright with pain, muscles cramp and twitch.

No time left to run. Prepare.

Four full waterskins; trail-biscuit; two buckets (empty); small pile of rags.

(A cholera sickroom, back in the city, back in the Decade of Woe – but no patient. No stench of gruel-thin shit and vomit.

These will come.)

Hands and knees, now. Drag cabinet in front of door. Cold sweat across face, down back. Pulse hammers beneath ribs. Jaw clenches, teeth grind. Fever or fear?

No difference.

Crawl to bed, claw at bootlaces. Hands like someone else's – someone old, close to death. Give up, back hunching. Lie back, limbs locked. A dying spider.

Nowhere else to run. Nowhere but memory.

The landlady has left her tenant's heart where she found it. Corner of the cupboard, left of the chimneybreast. Hanging above: one pair of ragged wool trousers. Worthless – which is why they're still here. Why the heart is still here, too.

"I'd have had him out sooner if I'd known, of course," says the landlady, leaning on the doorframe. Smoke drifts across the dim room from her cigarillo, picked out bright and momentarily white by the light thrown from the two unpatched panes of the garret's thin slash of a window. "This is a respectable boardinghouse." The hemp smells like sweet nettles; not a variant I recognise, something from beyond the city.

"Evidently." She's watching me, eyes narrowed; I glance at the mattress, stained like an artist's apron. The landlady's much better preserved and decorated than the rooms she rents. "Magick's not illegal, you know," I remind her. Not yet, anyway.

"Just because a thing isn't illegal doesn't mean we should all start doing it, Goodman Merrill," she chides.

"It is, however," I continue, "illegal to refuse a room to a tenant or evict them for political or religious reasons."

She sniffs. "That's unenforceable. Everyone knows it." She's right, too. Not enough rental stock to go around. I wonder how much she's charging for this closet.

She glares at me, challenging. *Bravado is always a mask,* my father used to tell me. "You look a little cerebral to be with the provost, Goodman," she continues.

Charming. "Sedition investigation office," I lie. "We leave the strong-arm stuff to the youngsters."

That's not strictly untrue. Emmelyne has been dragging the best of her first-wave recruits upstairs over the last few years, giving them roles that my father would recognise as a thieftaker's remit, and a thieftaker's alone. The provost was founded to "make justice accountable to law", as the Mayor put it at the time. Independent operators – thieftakers, like my father, engaged by the public to remove public menaces – had been unaccountable to anyone but those who paid. Sometimes not even to them.

So the Mayoral Council claimed monopoly on justice, and an exhausted city was glad to hand it to them. In the novellas I read as a youth, thieftaker characters stopped being heroes, became something more ambiguous. The lines on my father's forehead deepened in sympathy, as if the stories were being scratched into his flesh.

"Sedition?" She makes a moue of disgust. "What has that" – she points at the heart with an accusatory finger, long lacquered nail glistening like arterial blood in the wan light – "to do with sedition?"

"If I knew that, goodlady, I'd already have left you in peace." I placate her, trying to recall my father's advice. Years of shadowing him, half unwilling understudy, half disarming prop: a wheezing sickly boy, pockets stuffed with lurid novellas from the seedy bookstores of the Buchland print district. *They'll say things in front of an innocent that they'd never spill in front of me alone, boy.* I have no son. I am not my father. I can only imitate him, try to reproduce his effortless deceits and flatteries. Here, at least, the expansion of the provost under Emmelyne provides a useful mask; their authority, as yet, remains largely unquestioned in this part of the city.

Unlike that of the thieftaker.

I nod at the heart in the shade of its cupboard corner. "Have you seen one of these before?"

"No!" She looks horrified, digs in her bag for another cigarillo. "I'm very careful when interviewing tenants. Goodman Richell" – she nods toward the mattress, as if it contained her former tenant's essence – "he seemed like a good sort. A *local* man. You understand me." A raised eyebrow. "Hard working. Dockyards. Long shifts, he'd do." She looks thoughtful. "Kept himself to himself, perhaps, but always paid his rent on time." A shrug. "But no, I've never seen one of... one of *those*. Before now."

"Then what makes you think it's a thing of magick?" I ask her.

"Who'd want it as a good luck piece? Or a work of art? It's revolting." She frowns. "It looks *wrong*."

She's right. The heart, bristling with shipnails and dressmaking pins, looks as if the world hasn't quite allowed it to become part of the natural accepted order of things. At the same time, there's something familiar, like a memory of a fever-dream. Maybe it's just this garret I remember, or one similar... though I feel sure there were never so many garrets as grim as this one in the days when I followed my father.

"So Goodman Richell skipped out on his rent?" I ask to break the silence.

"No," she concedes, puzzled. "Paid in advance on Sunday, like always. Didn't see him all day Monday. Came up to bring him a letter that came for him this morning, and" – she points at the mattress – "well, there you see it. Gone." Cunning haunts her eyes. "Breach of contract to vacate without notice, though. I'll be keeping his deposit."

"Naturally," I say, for want of anything better. "Bring me the letter, please."

"The letter?" She stammers, looks like I've slapped her. "I threw it out this morning when I found he'd gone."

Did you, now.

"I'll have a look through your midden after I'm done here, then."

She feigns contemplation. "I might be thinking of the wrong letter. Let me go and have a look." She goes downstairs, leaves me alone. I slip on a leather glove, lift the mattress, then move across to the cupboard, prodding for hidden hatches or false panels. Nothing. Just the desiccated heart, studded with ironmongery, dried to a leathery brown. I pick it up; the pressure of my gloved fingers forces a faint wheeze from the ventricles.

I'm wrapping it in a nearly-clean kerchief as the landlady returns, breathless from the stairs. She has the letter. "I was thinking of a different one entirely!" Her laugh is shrill; her eyes dart. The back of the envelope is damp and slightly rippled. She has steamed it open. I tuck it into my jacket pocket.

"Thank you, goodlady," I tell her. "You're certain you've not seen the like of the heart before?"

"Never, I promise you! This is a respectable establishment," she reiterates. I wonder how many of her rooms are for rent on an hourly rate. She's too well-fed, too comfortable in her righteousness, to not be making far more than the official weekly rate for a dozen cubbyholes like this.

"But one hears rumours, of course," she continues, eager to regain my favour after her blunder with the letter. "From other landlords. Queer things left in abandoned rooms, especially by –" Another word bitten off unsaid. I prefer the poor to those who prey upon them. At least the poor are forthright about who they hate, and why. "Well, one just doesn't expect it from *normal* people." She sniffs again. "My Geffrey, he'd have been appalled to see the state of this city. Everything he fought for, all those brave citizens who gave their lives during the Decade. No one seems to care."

"Troubled times, goodlady," I concede, moving for the staircase. I want to tell her about her own part in the state of the city, but I know she hasn't the ears to hear it.

Back at my lodgings, Fentham is cowering in a corner by the bookcase, fur fluffed out in anger. I've had visitors while I was out. This happens when you're the thieftaker.

I move around my study, looking carefully, not touching anything. My disorder is deliberate; another strategy passed down from my father. There are finger streaks in the dust on the bookshelves. The desk drawers have been opened, but rifled only casually. A few mementos on the desktop have been moved. On the blotter rests something new: another heart, like the one in my jacket pocket.

I sit down to smoke and think, the hemp's mock solace seeping through me. Fentham skulks from the corner, leaps onto the desk and pours himself into my lap. He flexes with pleasure. I wince. His claws need trimming again.

Time was I'd find my lodgings rifled once a month, at least. Thieftaking has always been a precarious business, a profession that exists on the sufferance of power. You live only for as long as you are more useful to the people alive. To have a long career, you have to learn to see when the power is shifting, and to follow it.

The thieftaker works – worked – for the people, like a freelance prototype of the provost. That remit sometimes aligned with the interests of the crown, or the Admiralty, or the church. It rarely opposed them – but when it did, the people's support was the thieftaker's protection. The Admiralty appreciated the value of someone who'd do the jobs they considered too small, too fiddly.

But they were too busy playing god on the shores of the Mittlemeer to see their influence waning at home. By the time the Decade of Woe was over, my father's contracts came almost exclusively from the Mayoral Committee – as have mine, since he died and left me to fill his shoes. Three years, and they've dwindled down to this: chasing after mumbo-jumbo for the Mayor's puppeteer.

I have watched the Mayor's power wane, but I cannot follow the trail. It hasn't moved so much as diffused. No one knows who runs this city now. The only certainty is that the more someone believes it to be them, the more likely they are to act as if this were true.

This is a bad time to be a thieftaker. It is a bad time to be working for the Mayor.

I am doing both. Near enough.

Fentham protests my inattention. I scratch behind his ear as I stare at the heart on my desk, then fish out the one from the boardinghouse and unwrap it for comparison. There's not much in it, beyond the pattern of the nails and pins. From what little I know of magick, that indicates little more than the maker's whimsy. Maybe madness. Both hearts are too withered to identify. I want to believe they're pig hearts. That's harder than I'd like it to be.

There is a knock at my door. Fentham arches and spits, bolts for his corner.

"It's open," I call.

The door yawns, admitting Emmelyne. A grey wool cloak covers the armour of the Mayoral Guard, but does little to disguise its bulk. She looks at my desk, nods at the hearts.

"Two already," she observes. "The Mayor will be pleased."

I doubt he'll find out, actually, or that he knows anything about the hearts. Emmelyne does more mayoral legwork than the Mayor has the time or inclination to generate.

"He might not be," I reply. "I found that one at a boardinghouse in Easterny. The other was here waiting for me when I got in."

"Oh, really?" She gives me an unreadable look. "From an informant?"

"Yes," I lie. "I still have a few."

"I hadn't noticed a shortage." Emmelyne smiles, and as always I'm left wondering how sharp the teeth behind those haughty lips might be, and when they might bite. I am useful to her – or perhaps to the Mayor – right now. But for how long?

"So where are they coming from?" Emmelyne doesn't waste time.

"No idea yet," I tell her, and recount my boardinghouse experience. Everything except the letter.

"Dogman magick, is it?" She picks up the boardinghouse heart, lifting it with confident fingers as her lips curl with contempt. "Those vermin will believe anything." Emmelyne hates dogmen, and doesn't believe in magick. The former stance is more common than the latter.

"We can't have this carry on, Merrill. Citizens vanishing, these things turning up in their place. Doesn't look good, does it?"

"If you believe in magick, I suppose not," I venture. She glares at me, her eyes like flint.

"It's charlatanism, Merrill. You know that as well as I do." I think it, but I don't know it. "But the poor believe in it, and they're disappearing. Once the press gets hold of it –"

I show her a ragged broadsheet I peeled from an Easterney hoarding.

She scans, curses. "There's a lynch mob waiting for a wet and troubled day." She leans over the desk toward me. "The Mayor doesn't like mobs, Merrill. They have a tendency to look for fresh targets. Find where those hearts are coming from. Soon." She turns, heads for the door.

"We haven't agreed a fee for this investigation," I point out.

"We can talk about what your work's worth once you've done it," she says, without turning.

The door slams behind her.

Loengg's apothecary has been in business longer than I've been alive. My father would come here for advice on cases involving magick, stand in this stinking backstreet until Loengg sent out his boy. I squint at the peak of the roofs opposite, where the terraces huddle against the dockyard wall. Sullen gulls and crows return my stare from their perches among the barbed wire. A large rat, fat with fish scraps from the market middens, slinks blithely southwards along the gutter.

"The master will see you now." Loengg's boy at my elbow. He looks no different to the day I first saw him, years ago, doing my best not to cower in my father's shadow. He looks up at me, his soft brown eyes empty, unreadable. He walks back into the squat little house without a word. I follow. I remember the way.

Loengg's loft is long and narrow, like all the houses in Portsee. The bare boards are strewn with curios and novelties: the skulls of unrecognisable animals; jagged fists of coloured glass or crystal; mouldering tomes bound in leather and snakeskin; small piles of foreign coinage. Each object or set of objects stands in a geometric shape drawn in chalk upon the floor. The shapes are connected with chalk lines, some perfectly straight, some curving in ways the eye refuses to follow. Ornate sigils and words from unfamiliar languages lurk in the voids between, and each line leads – inexorably – to Loengg himself, sitting cross-legged on the floor at the window end of the loft. Behind him the midmorning sun, struggling over the dockyard wall across the street, seeps through the milky glass. Loengg's head is haloed; the light turns his thin cloud of grey hair into a nimbus. I suspect this is why I had to wait. My father thought dabblers in magick to be frauds, but he respected their grasp of showmanship.

"Thieftaker's son," he says, his voice as thin as his gaunt limbs and hollow, cadaverous face. "Not seen you in years." His eyes are bright white against the tallow of his skin, their nigh-black centres sliding around like a lunatic's. Arrayed on the floor beside him are a little spirit-lamp, a steel spoon with a blackened bowl, a glass dropper, a large dressmaker's needle. My father used to say that Loengg's best claim to magickal aptitude was the fact that the poppytar hadn't yet killed him. Looking at him now, I wonder if the poppy isn't in fact the source of his uncanny longevity. There is no flesh to Loengg, no meat. He's a sketch in curved bone and knotted sinew.

"The thieftaker's son is now the thieftaker," I tell him. "For whatever that's worth."

Loengg emits a wheezing chuckle. "Worth knowing, innit?" He squints at me, his angular face sharpened further by a sudden flash of focus. "Who does the thieftaker work for, though? That's more worth knowing."

"For the Mayor, for now."

"For the Mayor, or for those who work for the Mayor?" he asks, sly.

"Is there a difference?" I return.

A feral grin. "Thieftaker should know that. Or is that what he came here to ask?"

"What would you tell me if it was?"

He meets my eyes. "She's poison, that one."

There's always a sense that Loengg knows more than he's letting on. I recall my father's manner with him: curt, businesslike. I draw the boardinghouse heart from my pocket, unwrap it. "I came to ask about this."

Loengg's eyes narrow slightly, but there is no surprise in them. "What you wanna know of the strongmeat?"

"What is it for?"

"Strength charm. Dogman magick." His grasping hand beckons. I step toward him, mindful not to tread on the lines and symbols, pass him the grisly lump. "Makes the heart stronger." A physickal stimulant, then? That might make sense. Richell was a dockworker, doing long hours...

"Are they true magick, though? Not just hedge-witch charms?" Every street corner in the city has a hedge-witch sat on a blanket strewn with potions, herb bundles and cantrips. Reassurance retains its market value.

Loengg laughs again. "You forget what I tell your father so many times?" He taps his temple with a skeletal finger. "Magick – all magick – found here." He gestures at the heart, now resting on the floor in front of him. "Strongmeat is only a key."

This makes about as much sense as Loengg has ever made. "How does it work?" I ask.

Loengg makes a clicking sound with his throat, reaches behind him and brings forward a small sharp knife. I try my best not to flinch. He lifts the heart in his other hand, cuts neatly into the largest chamber. There's a musty smell of decay, like an abandoned butcher's shop. He puts down the knife, worms his fingers into the leathery flesh, tugs something out.

"Gotta be custom made, see." He holds out a long narrow strip of paper, stained in queasy pinks and browns. Along it are written a long string of characters in the dogmen's curious and impenetrable script, ending with the Anglic letters that spell out the name *Harmann Richell*. "Like an envelope for a letter, no?" He taps his head again.

"Magick comes from here. Your name calls it out, connects you to it."

I don't understand any of this. My father would say that it's all charlatanry, a manipulation of the client's willingness to believe. Which doesn't preclude them getting the results they've asked for, oddly; hedge-witches are rarely short of custom.

"Loengg," I ask, "who makes these? Where do they come from?"

"You ask your bosslady?"

"She doesn't know. That's why I'm here."

Loengg shakes his head, as if at a failing student. "Many folk make 'em." He jerks a bony thumb across his shoulder. "Ask for strongmeat in dockyard markets, you find it soon enough." He smiles again. "Less it find you first."

"What do you mean?" I snap. Loengg's boy tenses, but his master raises a calming hand in his direction.

"What I mean is what I know. The strongmeat seeks the thieftaker more than the thieftaker seeks the strongmeat." He peers at me intently. "Some find you already, no?" How does he know? Is he guessing? I keep my face immobile. Loengg shows his yellowy teeth, limned with decay. "I'm no more help to you now." He points at the floor, tracing a long looping line from his toes to mine. "Maybe your turn to help, huh? Find your path."

I'm suddenly tired, irritated. "And what will be at the end of my path, Loengg?"

"Ain't my path to walk, is it?"

I thank Loengg through gritted teeth, let his boy lead me back to the filthy street. I return to my lodgings, cut open the heart that was left for me. The strip of paper hidden within ends with my name, scratched out by a crude but careful hand.

I open the letter that arrived for Richell. What – if anything – had the landlady kept from it? All it contains now is a single sheet of fine onionskin paper, folded neatly in half. On one folded-in face is written only two words in shaky copperplate.

Come home.

I stand up, go out.

I wander the city for hours, looking anywhere but where the answers might be found. I spot Emmelyne on the Gilthall Walk, where Portsee blends into the university quarter. She's clearing out a poppytar den: she watches, arms crossed, from the middle of the street as her Guards toss gaunt students, grizzled amputee sailors and a couple of burnt-out dogmen into the gutter.

I try to vanish among the crowd of onlookers, but her eye is keen, her voice strident. "See? Wherever we find the dogs, Merrill, we find corruption," she calls across the street, teeth flashing in triumph. Some of the crowd turn surly glares my way. "How goes your own quest?"

I close the distance between us. Proximity is risky, but so is having the chief of the Mayoral Guard shout your name across a riot waiting to happen. She's not afraid. She sweeps her gaze across the crowd, challenging, like flintsparks over oil-soaked kindling.

"I have some leads," I tell her. It might even be true.

"I knew I could rely on you, Merrill." Somewhere inside, my father laughs to hear this. She watches as one of the old sailors retches a thin yellow trail of bile onto the cobbles. "You're helping us make a difference."

"Lucky me." It slips out before I have time to think.

Emmelyne shakes her head, staring expectantly at me. It's the same look Loengg gave me, the same look the landlady gave me, the same look that follows me through the markets and down the alleyways, along the parades and promenades. Everyone expects me to know what's going on.

I'm supposed to be the thieftaker, after all.

"What do you want from me, Emmelyne?" I ask, my

voice dull from hemp and lack of sleep.

She smiles, sly. "It's not about what I want. I work for the Mayor, remember? For the good of the city."

"I'm not sure I believe that fairytale any more," I say.

"You don't have to believe a fairytale to understand its moral, Merrill." She giggles at her accidental rhyme, and I wonder, not for the first time, how sane she really is. Or whether it's me that has the problem.

Her steel-clad arm slips round my shoulders, a cold embrace. "And where do your leads point you, Goodman Thieftaker?"

"Need to follow some things up at the dockyard."

"The dockyard?" Her eyes widen with feigned little-girl wonder. "Whatever might you find there, Merrill?"

"I don't know until I go."

"Don't you?" She leans in close; faint smell of rust and sweat from her mailshirt. "Better go soon, then. Hmm?" Her eyes are flint again. I jerk a nod, slip out from under her arm and away.

I'm almost clear when she commends me loudly to the thickening mob. I'm the Mayor's left hand, to hear her tell it; helping the Guard stem the tide of foreign vice in the city.

I slip away, the small of my back itching in anticipation of a knifethrust that doesn't come.

Not yet.

It's nearly Firstwatch. A nail-clipping moon hangs wanly in the dark before dawn, but the dockyard market still seethes, as it does all day and all night. Every city has a market where you can buy – so you'll be told – anything that you can name. It's true here, now. Maybe it's true everywhere it's said.

I wish I'd travelled, when I had the chance.

Still, thanks to Loengg I can name what I need. I stalk the smoky dark between the stalls. The smells: rotting fish guts; decaying vegetables; a dark exotic note of tobacco cutting through the chords of hemp and hash. Shit; fear; anger. Money. The sounds: night-merchant banter, a polyglot babble of fragmented conversation that connects the stalls and booths and barrows together like the knots of a fisherman's net, making of them an invisible organism in constant communication with itself. They say that news of an unpopular face can cross the whole market in less time than a thrown rock takes to fall to ground.

This, too, is true. I am known here. The thieftaker is always known in places like this. The old pacts promise his safety; this is truce ground, of a sort. I'm not sure how strong that truce remains. It held for my father, even after two very high-profile seizings made right here in the market.

I am not my father. And no one ever steps into the same market twice.

The dogman is an old cur, oldest in the chain of five I've spoken to. Rheumy eyes in a face creased from long years squinting into the sun at sea. Smile like a slash in a sack of grain.

"I remember you," he growls. "Merrill. Your father was..." He nods, slowly and deliberately, as if to someone watching from behind me. I will myself to stand loose, to keep smiling, but be ready to move.

Nothing happens.

"Man of your profession shouldn't be so nervous round here. Or ain't that so no more?" He smirks. "Don't remember me, do you? Well, you were young. What you want, Thieftaker?"

I jerk my chin. "Your colleague back there tells me you have the strongmeat."

"That so? You want some, do you?"

"I want to know where it comes from."

He laughs. His thick filed-down canines are pitted with dark brown grooves. "You haven't guessed yet?"

"I have theories."

"You always had your theories. Swear you told me

more stories than I ever told you, back then." He looks thoughtful. "Your old man, he was a practical bloke."

"I am not my father."

"You think I don't know that?" He leans back in his creaking chair. His stall of gimcracks and nick-nacks is a flotsam-strewn river of moth-eaten navy felt, rippling motionless between us. "You get the one you were sent?"

Ah. "I did."

"And?"

I grope for an answer. Settle for simplicity. "It was dead." The dogman frowns. "Dried up," I continue, shrugging. "I don't know what you want me to say." He won't believe that, but it's true.

"What does that mean, Merrill," he asks, very quietly. "Why was there a dried out strength charm with your name in it?"

I don't know. "A warning," I say, sounding more certain than I am.

He rolls his eyes, leans forward, elbows on his knees. "Why do you think you weren't sent a fresh one?"

"Why would I need one?"

"Exactly." He nods once, sharply. I nod back. The silence between us lets the babble back in. We're still looking at each other.

He breaks the silence: "You don't get it, do you?" Takes my silence for assent: "You can only get the names in when the hearts are fresh, Thieftaker. Otherwise the magic won't work. It was dried out because it was used up."

"But *my* name was in there. Who could have used it?" I ask.

He blinks, once. It hits me. He nods again.

"How long," I whisper.

"Since before you could talk, boy." He looks sorry, or at least sympathetic. But there's something else in his eyes, too. A seeking. "One of my lads, he makes you up a fresh one every week."

"Why?" I ask, but I already know.

"My debt to your old man, wasn't it? Wanted you to grow up tough and smart, didn't he?"

Because a thieftaker must be strong, and because I must be the thieftaker. But his logic was wrong from the start, I remind myself, the numb satisfaction of self-pity flowing through me like poppytar. The first statement precludes the first. It always has done.

"It didn't work," I tell him.

"You reckon?" The old dogman snorts, shaking his head. "I saw you as a baby. Sickly mewling thing you were, too." His voice softens, moistened at the edges by something like compassion. "Your father was a good bloke, Thieftaker. Not just 'cause he saved my bacon, either. He hated having to leave you with a wetnurse, y'know."

"He might have considered that before he sent my mother away."

The dogman bows his head. The silence stretches out, the susurrus of commerce seeping through.

"Your old man always played us dogmen fair, Thieftaker. Not many did, and less do now. But times being what they are –" He gropes for words. "Look, you owe us nothing, right? The strongmeat, that's between me and your old man, a personal thing. You don't need to worry on that score. But people round here, well, they don't see you round much, you know? Except when the Mayor's whip-bitch throws you a rotten fish she can't be bothered to chew."

"No one else is hiring," I tell him. It's true enough.

"Aye, I know," he says, placatory, his hands out, fingers spread. "It's just that –" That nervous pause again. I watch the dogman look furtively left and right, feel my father watching from somewhere behind me. "There's a feeling in some parts of the city," he says slowly, watching my face, "that working for the Mayor might become rather more hazardous in the near future."

"Are you threatening me?"

He growls a curse, turns his head and spits. "No, Thieftaker. I'm trying to keep you safe. Why would I stop now?"

The door of my lodgings hangs open, an exhalation of threat. I go inside, stepping over the books thrown to the floor: paper birds with broken leather wings. Little looks to be missing. This is a demonstration. I call for Fentham, wander through to my bedroom. Emmelyne sits on my unmade bed, leafing through one of my father's diaries.

"Looks like you had visitors again, Merrill."

"Yes," I say. "I wonder who it might have been." I'm tired; my sarcasm lacks teeth.

"The door was open when I arrived."

"I'm sure it was." I turn my back on her, walk back through to the wreck of my study. "I'd love to talk shop, but I have packing to do." Behind me, I hear her toss the diary to the floor, get to her feet.

"Packing? Where are you going, Merrill?"

"Does it matter?"

She grabs my upper arm, her fingers strong from years of swordplay. "Yes, it matters," she hisses. "Thieftaker you may be, but as a citizen you're still subject to the Mayor." That smile again; vulpine. "I like knowing what you're up to."

"When I'm not doing your bidding, I'm usually sat here reading. Which is most of the time." I sound petulant, feel my strength ebb and pulse. Imagine a heart, still fresh and firm, its nails and pins still bright from the forge, sat somewhere in the city, twitching around a ribbon of parchment with my name scrawled across it.

"If you made more of yourself, Merrill, I might drop more work in your lap. You're the thieftaker, for fuck's sake! Your father –"

I round on her, grabbing the wrist of the hand on my arm. There's a fury in my eyes that Emmelyne flinches from.

She's never flinched from me before. Her pupils shrink to tiny points as I stare into them.

"I. Am. Not. My. Father," I say, biting down on each word. I release her wrist, turn away again. I look at my desk, wonder what to take with me. Whether I should take any of it.

"That's plain enough," she says, her voice unsteady. I feel a tiny spark of triumph aglow in my chest, the glory of power exercised successfully. It's a candle in a cold room; I understand, perhaps for the first time, how my father might have come to love his work. "He'd be ashamed to see you now," she continues, her voice climbing. "Giving up. After everything he did for you. Thieftakers inherit the post, Merrill. You can't walk away from that."

Oh, but I can. "How long have you known?" I ask her. I'm calm, now. Still empty, still tired. But it's like someone opened a door and let a breeze blow through me.

"About your little problem? Years," she says. "Part of my briefing when I took the post. Mayoral Council always assumed you knew."

"So why set me to investigate?"

She picks up an overturned chair, sits down with a sigh. "Think of it as a test. Seeing if you held any lingering loyalties that had outlived their era."

"Checking the corpse for a pulse, in other words."

She shrugs. "If you like."

I step behind my desk, tug open the top drawers. The junk of a wasted life looks out.

"Where will you go, Merrill?" She's calm, but the steel edge of command still rings in her words.

"The mainland. I don't know." I don't know.

"You can't leave the city, Merrill. You're the thieftaker. You're part of the machine, an organ in the body." She stands up again, starts pacing, shifts to her drill-sergeant voice. "The city has changed, and changed for the worse. You've seen the markets, the slums. The dogmen, they're ungovernable. They don't know their place. We need you here. Doing the job your father handed down to you." She stops pacing, glances at me. "You know why your father came to work for the Mayor."

I do know. I've read all his diaries – not just the ones I didn't destroy. It wasn't why she thinks it was. My father wanted to balance the Mayor's power, not to bolster it.

He failed. And he knew his son was weak, a dreamer. So he made his bargain with the dogmen. Asked them to make me strong, so I might protect them.

He never asked *me*. Never asked me about anything, never explained. I owe him nothing, owe the city nothing.

So I say nothing, lift a few trinkets from my drawers.

"Damn it, Merrill," she sighs, suddenly human. "Why can't you accept your place in the grand scheme of things?"

I slam the drawer shut. "Because it's a lie. A fiction." I glance at my bookshelves. I'll be loath to leave them.

"You can never come back." It's not a threat, but a statement of fact.

"I know," I tell her.

"You know what will happen to you, once you're outside? Once the strongmeat can't reach you?" Her voice is quiet, now. "Hinterland patrols found your Goodman Richell, you know, and some others before him. Dead, dried out like those filthy hearts. Stretched out in the dirt under a gorse bush, like he'd just been cut off the rack."

"I thought you didn't believe in magick," I mutter. Thought I didn't, either.

She rolls her eyes. "You've never really grasped how politics work outside of your tawdry novellas, have you?" She steps toward me, a hand extended. "Stay, Merrill. Let us help you. Let *me* help you. I'll make sure you get the latest scuttle from the Guard's informers. We'll lean on the dogmen, wean you off the magick slowly. Set you free. What do you say?"

I stare at her scar-tracked hand, thinking back to the

old dogman's warnings, to Loengg's hedge-witch metaphysicks. I don't know who to trust. *Charlatanry*, mutters my father's memory, and my head believes him, wants to believe him.

My heart is no longer so sure.

"I must finish packing," I tell her, opening a lower drawer. "If you'll excuse me, please."

Emmelyne says nothing. I look up a few minutes later, and she's gone. Fentham, his coat slick with drizzle and limned with the pre-dawn light, slinks in through the door from the street, accompanied by the sounds of the city shaking itself awake.

I carry on packing all the things that matter most to me. It doesn't take long.

I float upward through a rouge ocean. The deep long boom of a war-galleon's pace drum calls me, louder, clearer. So close I can feel it. My ribs twitch to its beat.

I breathe in, but do not drown. Cool air flows into me. The taste of stale sweat sings sharp over other, darker odours. I don't gag. My stomach is a clenched thing, dry and empty, growling quietly for sustenance after a long silence.

There is birdsong. I open my eyes a crack; light pours in, white agony. I blink away the tears. A rasping half-word tries to clamber from my throat.

A knock at the door. Desultory, expecting to go answered. Muffled whispers from the corridor outside. I roll onto my side, away from the slat-shuttered window and its blades of brightness, opens my eyes again to look around the room. Not looking forward to cleaning that up.

Knock-knock-knock.

"Hello," I say, experimentally. I sound like a starving crow.

"Goodman Merrill?" The innkeeper. I wonder if he sent the letter to Loengg. I wonder whether it matters, decide that it does.

"Goodman Merrill, are you all right?"

I close my eyes again, breathe deep and slow before answering.

"I'm alive," I croak, as if to see how it feels.

It's true enough.

Entr'acte

Simon Morden

I discovered that I'd become a parody of myself. Not that I could remember when I'd started drinking whiskey, or even when I'd started putting an e in whiskey: just that when the time came for me to hurriedly clear my desk, make the client believe if just for a moment, that they were dealing with a professional problem-solver rather than some play-acting fool – it was a half bottle of Jim Bean and an empty shotglass that I tidied away.

I had slatted blinds I could wind open and shut, a bentwood hat stand and steel filing cabinet. About the only original feature I didn't have was a snub-nosed .35, because having ballistic weaponry in a sealed pressure dome on the Moon was simply nuts. My heat was a taser, a little yellow and black plastic thing that looked like a child's toy. I still wore it in a shoulder holster over a crisp white shirt and under a jacket. I was a masquerade, that was all. There was nothing else behind the curtain.

My client was a woman: Earth-born, late-twenties, skin and facial features Mogadishu by way of the Levant. She dressed like almost everyone did, men and women: a one-piece, one-colour coverall, easy to clean – because despite every effort, gunmetal-grey dust got everywhere – and some sort of belt or bag to tote personal effects around. She hesitated outside the door: I could see her shadow on the wall behind her, see the top of her head on the screen on my desk via the camera perched, mosquito-like, on the doorframe.

She hesitated because the door had a handle, like a regular door would back on Earth. She searched the wall for the controls, the door for an airtight bulkhead wheel, some sort of press-button intercom. She'd have had to have been up here a long time to forget to just knock and enter.

"Mr Harrison?"

My name was on the door, but it didn't hurt to check. I waved my hand at the chair opposite. I didn't have to take time to get into character. I was the character.

"Virgil, please, Mrs Rached. Can I get you a coffee?"

Look at me: I had a coffee machine on top of the filing cabinet. I had all the stage props.

She turned me down, which was probably a good thing, as I only know how to make coffee one way, and if she'd got any more strung-out, she would have snapped. She sat, perched on the very edge of the chair, balanced in the one-sixth gravity in a way that confirmed she'd been away from home for a very long time. But she was nervous. Her dark eyes wouldn't settle, and neither would her hands, fluttering like moths before the flame.

"Why don't you tell me what this is all about?"

I could have used the screen, set it to record everything. I'd done that already, secretly, and she wasn't paying me to psychoanalyse her. I made a show of getting out a notebook, folding back the dog-eared pages filled with my spiky writing, reaching into my jacket for a ball-point pen, clicking it and laying it in front of me, while behind me, a rocket was taking off, laser-assisted, scattered light slanting sideways through the blinds. It was a projection and we were ten metres below the regolith – but it was real-time, looking towards Plaskett's central peak.

"My husband's missing," she said.

I picked up my pen and I wrote missing in capitals. People didn't go missing on the Moon. At least, when they did, they turned up again quickly enough not to need me to find them. I underlined the single word I'd written, once, twice, and laid the pen down.

"And you've...?"

The Moon hasn't got a government, so everything's handled by the corporations that have set up shop here.

There are no judges, no juries, no prisons, no guards and no parole. And definitely no cops. When bad stuff happens, the corporations handle it. Resources are hard won, expensive, rare. Every last gram of it gets tracked. And that includes people. Everyone is someone's employee. Except me.

"No one knows where he is."

Not that there's zero cooperation between the corporations' heads of security: they talk to each other all the time. Yes, they're here to earn a buck, but keeping it tight in a place where a simple hole in the wall can ruin your day is in everyone's best interest. So for this guy's employers to have lost track of him had to mean that he'd really gone off the map. Suits get counted daily, and they all have transponders. Rovers likewise and more so. Passenger manifests are all searchable. Stowaways show up due to the discrepancy between mass and fuel use. If he hadn't gone outside and he hadn't gone back to Earth, then he was somewhere in the tunnels and domes of the Moon – where every litre of oxygen, every cc of water, every kilo of food was inventoried. Each time the guy went to the john, some computer somewhere would record it. There was, literally, figuratively and even metaphorically, nowhere to hide.

"Okay, Mrs Rached. I'm going to need some details."

She broke into a relieved white smile. Maybe she thought I was going to tell her to stop wasting my time. Maybe she thought I was going to sense some corporate cover-up and decline to handle the case. Maybe – I don't know – maybe she thought I was a joke, a man who set himself up as a private investigator on a world where everything is so tightly controlled and so closely observed that there's almost nothing to be discovered that isn't already in plain sight.

"Call me Leila," she said.

Culture-transplants are strange things. Festivals – Hanukkah, Eid, Christmas, Divali – they've all made it up here, but they've changed, the traditions associated with them morphed into something peculiarly lunar. Not so chanoyu. The chashitsu had been brought whole from Earth and installed with the utmost care in the JAXA facilities in Kepler, by their head of security, Tetsuya Fujikawa. The Way of Tea was his thing. God forbid if you took the ceremony with less than the utmost sincerity. It wasn't that Fujikawa would shove you head-first out into the vacuum, but those who thought chanoyu quaint or superfluous, or worse, a ridiculous waste of four hours? They never prospered.

So when I received an invitation to take tea with him, I put on my best suit and hitched a ride on a Tata hopper that was heading to the equator. My best suit was an old, patched Orlan. It held together just fine, even if the instruction book came in Russian. I could change the filters, keep the air tanks full and stop the visor from fogging. It was fine as long I didn't have to go hiking across a mare.

Now this was the thing: Leila's husband didn't work for JAXA. She'd told me everything that was on his employment record, and I wasn't so slack to take it on trust. I'd checked both him and her as thoroughly as I would my usual type of client – one indignant half of a failing relationship. Mohammed Rached had worked for McDonnell, for EADS, a brief stint with Infinite Resources and then back to EADS. No Mitsubishi Heavy Industries or IHI. I was at a loss to explain why Fujikawa wanted to talk to me – at least, I assumed he wanted to talk – but when his invitation arrived in my inbox, I knew I'd be a fool to refuse it.

The Indians dropped me off on the edge of Kepler, before coasting away towards Tata's helium-three mines, and I walked to the nearest airlock. I say walked, but you don't really walk on the Moon, no matter what the song says. You do that skipping motion and try not to break anything. Once inside, I hoovered my suit down and stowed it in a locker. First rule of lunar living: keep the dust out. By the time the inner door had cycled, there was someone there to escort me to the chashitsu. JAXA had tunnelled themselves a regular warren in the broken rock of the crater wall, and the base was marked by signs in kanji. If it hadn't been for the pictograms, I'd have been completely lost.

In lieu of the roji, there was an extra door separating the chashitsu from the main corridor. It was a small space, barely wide enough for the bench, or for the partially-open cupboard facing it. Nothing here was left ajar without good reason, so I looked inside, and found several kimonos, sealed inside shrink-wrap plastic sleeves.

I'm no expert, but I knew enough not to disgrace myself. I picked a dark blue kimono, and wore it over my under-suit layer. Tying the obi wasn't easy, but I cheated and knotted it at the front before easing it around to the back. I swapped my soft-soled pumps for zori, and waited. Waiting was part of the ritual, and I wish I could say it took a long time for me to empty my mind. It didn't. My character was indeed that thin.

The inner door opened and my ears popped with the increased pressure. It appeared I was to be the only guest, which was unusual: the ceremony was both time-consuming and resource-consuming. I was either being honoured, or warned off. I'd learn which soon enough. I shuffled in across the mats and assumed the kneeling seiza position which, trust me, is a lot easier to maintain in one-sixth gravity.

I had a moment to look at the scroll in the alcove, the paper riffling slightly in the cycling air. It held a single kanji character, square and vaguely threatening. It looked like a stylised face, and I did my best to memorise its shape. As far as I knew, Fujikawa painted the scrolls himself, fresh for every ceremony, so it was going to be relevant somehow.

He was a small man, bird-like. His motions, as befitted his mastery of chanoyu, were precise and practised. He did everything in order, and I tried to keep up. His face, poker-straight throughout, gave nothing away as to whether I'd displeased him in my responses. There were elements of theatre, devotion, ritual, hospitality and examination. I was being paid by the hour plus expenses, but I would have done it for nothing; this was something not to be missed.

We made it intact to the end. Tea was drunk. Food was eaten. Bows were made. I admired the bold and commanding brush strokes on his calligraphy, and he thanked me, asking if I knew the character.

"My knowledge of the kanji is very much in its infancy," I conceded.

Not so much infancy, as still-born, but I guessed that Fujikawa didn't want to hear a bald, exposed negative.

"Your eagerness to learn does you much credit, Mr Harrison. Your current investigations go well?"

In the time I'd had, I gathered a screed of data on Leila's husband. He'd been at the EADS shack up at Schwartzchild, with only company-sanctioned ways of getting out when he'd vanished. I'd talked to Lizabetta Raynaud, who'd told me that she couldn't work out where he'd gone and she wasn't going to waste any more company money in looking for him. To be honest, I was less interested in the mechanism than I was in the motive. Everyone up here was smart, and finding new ways of gaming the system faster than the bean counters and security chiefs could close the old ones down was a sport.

"Dr Rached's disappearance is most perplexing," I said.

Security talked to security. There was no reason not to share. What one employee could do one day, lots would be doing by the next. Fujikawa would be keenly interested in knowing how someone could walk out of a secure facility, and presumably walk into another, without being detected in either. There was a hole in the net, somewhere.

"You have talked to his former colleagues, of course."

It wasn't like there was a space bar where everyone

hung out at the end of the day. There were recreational outlets for the workers, but being on the Moon had more in common with being on an oil rig stuck in the middle of an ocean than it did a nine-to-five in some sprawling city down below. I'd talked to Leila, and I'd talked to Raynaud. That was it. In fact, it was pretty unusual for a husband and wife to be Lunarside together. I looked up from the tatami mat. That wasn't what Fujikawa was saying at all.

"You believe it'd be instructive?"

There it was. Fujikawa couldn't go poking around in another company's business. But I could. And not just EADS either. I knew roughly what McDonnell did, but Infinite Resources? They were a mining outfit, remotely prospecting asteroids, and hadn't turned a profit yet. There were clearly people with deep pockets behind it, and I was being steered in their particular direction.

"Your effort," said Fujikawa, "might reap surprising rewards."

He didn't need to have been seen with me – he could have sent a note, anonymous and discreet. Except, except... I took one last look at the scroll, bowed deeply and thanked him for inviting me. He bowed too, and I raised myself out of the kneeling position. I had something to go on, and something to be frightened of. Out of all the places on the Moon, this one room was unsurveilled. And if being overheard worried Fujikawa, it scared the crap out of me.

Looking at the books, Infinite Resources appeared to be a strange, shoe-string outfit, mostly subletting other, larger corporations' space. IR personnel had short-term contracts that were rarely renewed. They picked key expertise and used it, before spitting it out like flavourless gum. They paid really, really well. On the other hand, maintaining a series of small domes of their own away over on the Farside put a different expression on their public face.

Follow the money, they say, and they're right. Money,

sex, revenge: that's what it boils down to, even in the under-pressurised atmosphere of sealed environment. Sometimes it's all three, but greed is an addiction and money the drug that fuels it. I'm not immune, and I don't pretend to be. So I followed the trail – it's what I trained in. I was never a cop, never worked security, never strongarmed a perp or worked them over behind the van. I'm an accountant. I balance columns of figures. Fear me.

What I found was an obscene amount of money simply appearing in IR's coffers, year in, year out. A billion dollars. Two billion. A billion and a half. Their CEO was, without a doubt, a sharp operator, but there was nothing to suggest that it was either his own personal wealth, or he'd attracted the attention of a trillionaire philanthropist willing to shovel cash into the gaping maw of the future without the prospect of seeing a return in their lifetime. I could tell where the money was going, tallying probe launches with subcontractors' bills, making estimates of running costs and advertised expenditure. What I couldn't tell was where the money was coming from.

My hunch was that Rached had worked this out for himself, and decided that he was either going to tap that inexhaustible flow of wealth, or make a hamfisted attempt at blackmail. Either way, IR made the problem go away, quite literally. The next thing to do was poke around the Racheds' bank balance, but nothing seemed out of the ordinary. A standard credit check showed they'd neither taken on nor paid off any significant loans, and that there were no big ticket items like a house, a yacht or a tropical island on the books.

Leila was my client. I gave her a call to come to the office, telling her I wanted to update her. Again, the whiskey went away, but I fired up the coffee machine before she got there, brewing enough for two.

"Have you found something?"

Her breathless hope was endearing, but misplaced. I

was certain by now that we wouldn't be seeing her husband again. I wanted to sympathise with her, so I poured her a slow coffee and set it in front of her.

"What can you tell me about Infinite Resources?"

Answering a question with a question was kind of rude. I did it any way. I needed to know the pillow talk, the things that the numbers couldn't tell me. Had they discussed new beginnings, away from the bone-white, sterile Moon? Or had they talked about buying themselves a slice of the prospecting action?

"Mo worked for them for six months. The contract ended, he moved on."

That was lame, and she knew it. She tried to look apologetic, with a cute shrug and an open-handed offering of exactly nothing.

"C'mon, Leila, you've got more than that. I know what he was paid to do at IR, but what did he really do?"

I kicked back my chair and watched steam devils rise off the surface of my coffee. I could wait. After all, she was paying. Maybe I'd got too used to people lying to me to be able to tell when they were speaking the truth, but that wasn't really my problem. She floundered, protesting her and her husband's innocence, unaware for the moment that I shouldn't be talking to her like that. With her defences laid bare, I hit her with the old one-two.

"Did he ever show any interest in how IR made its money? Or did he refuse to discuss that?"

She stopped like she'd just run into a brick wall, cartoon-style, arms and legs splayed. Splat.

"He said it was none of our business. Why? What's wrong with IR?" My turn to shrug. I projected the numbers into the air between us and waved my hand through them.

"Infinite Resources is a private company, so it's got no shareholders to keep happy. There's a consortium behind them, Infinite Holdings, that seems to have Infinite Pockets. Ten billion dollars have been transferred to IR to IH over the last eight years. Infinite Holdings has no other sources of income. This, Leila, is what money laundering looks like."

Her face fell. She was far from dumb, and she knew what this meant.

"You think Mo was going to rat them out?"

No, that wasn't what I thought. There was no one else snooping around IR, no feds knocking on their door and asking to go through their books. Stealing from criminals was a high-risk endeavour, but it wasn't as if they could go to the law. Rached was going to help himself from the pot of ill-gotten gains.

Or rather, he already had, and they'd caught up with him. No point in attracting attention by taking him out while he was still working for IR. Much better to do it later. Seven and a half months later. There was nothing in his name, so it'd be in some digital safe somewhere, waiting for the heat to cool off. He wouldn't have wanted evidence lying around in electronic form, though. It would have been a randomised string of numbers in his head, twenty characters or more. A feat to remember, dangerously easy to forget. Much better written down.

"I'm going to need to search your hab," I said.

I'd have preferred Leila to wait outside, but standing in a corridor by the closed door of your own living quarters? Someone would have noticed, and now I suspected Rached of making off with some of IR's cash, I decided that being noticed was bad.

I did make her stand just inside by the controls while I toured the hab. It didn't take me long: one room, about five metres by four, and an alcove wet-room barely bigger than a coffin. Apart from the folddown double bed, and that there was just enough space to swing a cat without dashing its brains out simultaneously on all four walls, it was much like my hab. Which, in turn, was much like everyone else's, no matter how much they got paid.

Where to start? I knew all the hiding places because the lockers were standard issue, whether they rolled out, folded out or telescoped. What was I looking for? A scrap of paper with a line of numbers, carefully concealed in the seam of a jacket, or a digital image containing the access code in the background. It certainly wouldn't be in plain text on a public server. Perhaps on a private memory stick?

"If you thought your husband was hiding something, where would he think you'd look?"

It was an oblique question, but I didn't want to have to go through everything, both his and hers. And I was here to find IR's missing money, and maybe work out a way of giving it back before they came for Leila. Call me chivalrous – hell, call me whatever you want – but Leila was a good kid, and didn't deserve to share whatever had happened to Rached.

"I don't know. I mean, it's not like we have much." That was true. Those who live for any length of time on the Moon whittle their physical possessions down to virtually nothing. It's just easier that way. Boats get barnacles, but selenites are stream-lined vessels.

"Show me what he brought with him."

She opened a drawer, and stood back to let me wander my fingers across the measure of a man's life. There were brass trinkets and old photographs, scraps of cloth, and a dog-eared copy of The Prophet by Khalil Gibran. I'd heard of it, but never read it. I flipped through the book, smelling the spice-worn paper. I held it by the spine and gave it a little shake. Nothing fell out.

But when I put the book down again, it tried to open, a visible bow in the arc of the pages. You learn to trust these little signs, so I slipped my fingernail in and examined the text.

Leila pushed close, her head bending low over the words with which her husband had wooed her, the last two lines made her breath catch in her throat and a tiny whimper slipped away.

Beauty is eternity gazing at itself in a mirror / But you are eternity and you are the mirror

I was more interested in the pencil marks under particular letters: two on the first line, two on the third, and so on, until the eleventh line, where there were three. And then no more. All the letters, apart from o were in the range a to i. One to nine, plus zero. Twenty symbols in all. Twenty numbers. I told you I was good with numbers, and this was nothing more complicated than a bank's account and sort code, followed by what looked like a four-figure PIN.

I could check that. I could check it now on the computer in my pocket. But I didn't want to, not in front of Leila. I closed the book and slid it inside my jacket where it nestled next to my taser.

"It'll be in code, and I'll have to work on it. I'll let you know when I've cracked it."

She nodded meekly. A better man would have felt like a heel, and explained everything. That wasn't in my character, not the one I was playing. So I touched my finger to my brow in the absence of a hat to doff, and worked my way through the labyrinthine corridors back to my office.

I checked what I had, typed in the numbers and called up the account. There was a tricky moment with the personal question, but I knew enough about Leila's life to be able to guess it first time. The account held a metric tonne of cash, enough for two sensible people to retire comfortably and live without ostentation for the rest of their lives. In Rached's case, about seven months.

I gave Fujikawa a call, and we spoke only in circumlocutions.

"Mr Harrison. Have you deciphered the meaning of the *ma* character?"

I had, in all honesty, forgotten about it. But as I talked, I quickly sketched it from memory on a blank page in my notebook, and showed it to my screen.

"Work regarding that is in progress, Mr Fujikawa. But on another matter, some lost property has come into my possession, and I'd like to know the best way to return it to the owner."

Fujikawa looked down at his lap, deep in thought. I didn't interrupt. Eventually he raised his head, and nodded at his own sagacity.

"Quickly," he said.

My stomach knotted tighter than a spacesuit seal. Whatever fate had taken Mohammed Rached and threatened his widow, now hung over me.

"Thank you for your candour."

I cut the connection, and examined the results of my search. *Ma*. This wasn't straightforward translation. The characters had layers of meaning, and I was going to have to dig deep. Ma meant time, and more. One word caught my eye, one I didn't know, either in its original French, or its English counterpart: entr'acte, the interval between two acts of a play.

Was that where Fujikawa thought I was? If that was the case, I didn't want to hang around for the resolution of the plot. No way was I going to exit, stage left, pursued by a bear. If I was to placate the capricious gods of Infinite Resources, I needed to do it now.

You know at some point in the story, I'm going to get sandbagged and wake up in unfamiliar surroundings. This is that point. Of course it didn't matter that I'd behaved perfectly correctly throughout: I'd broken no laws, acted in the best interests of my client, and was as decent as my shabby, down-at-heel gumshoe persona would allow. I was written in as the fall guy, and a moment's inattention, a distracted thumbing of the door-release when I should have kept it firmly locked – that was all it took.

The next thing I knew, the barbs of someone else's taser impaled my lilywhite chest and a man I didn't recognise stood at the far end of the carbon fibre spirals. The next thing I knew after *that*, I was on the floor of a hopper, gliding over the rugged, pock-marked face of the Farside, while two spacesuit pilots ignored my return to consciousness.

I tried my hands, but my wrists were as cuffed as my ankles. I didn't have a gag, but since I was surrounded by a billion cubic kilometres of vacuum it didn't matter how loud I screamed for help. Nor was that the only problem. Even if I managed to free myself and overpower the two pilots, what kind of idiot deliberately attacks someone who's, at that moment, flying the goddamn ship? A desperate one, that's who, and I didn't know if I'd quite arrived at that station. Yet.

With my taser gone, I decided that I could still talk my way out of this. Give them the codes, let them have their cash, convince them that not only did I know nothing about Rached, I wasn't about to go on a fishing expedition either. Where IR got its funds from was a well far deeper and darker than I wanted to draw from. If Leila wanted her money back, too, that was fine by me, just as long as I kept breathing.

My surroundings offered me no immediate hope. I could probably kick my way out of the hull, but my hosts had forgotten to provide me with a spacesuit, so all I could really do was lie back and enjoy the ride, all the way to IR's domes in Thiessen. I played dead, hoping to overhear something of use from the pilots, but they spent the entire journey with their helmets on. Any words spoken between them were ones I couldn't hear, and it made for a really tedious trip. At least it gave me time to practice my speech, and meditate a little on the meaning of *ma*.

Restraints cut, I was escorted – politely but firmly – through an extendible airlock tube into the main dome. It didn't look like a super-villain's hideout, except for the uniforms, the busyness of the personnel, the incomprehensible instructions being barked over the tannoy, and the bizarrely complex machinery half-buried in the regolith, dead-centre under the highest point of the curved ceiling.

Okay, so it looked almost exactly like a super-villain's hideout. I was led around the circumference of the dome to a platform where jumpsuited techs monitored the status of whateverthehell the thing was. Stood behind them was a slight man, blue coveralls, but with a thousand-dollar haircut and so obviously in charge that I straightened my posture and walked a little smarter.

"Mr Harrison," he said over his shoulder, "what do you think?"

Honestly, I had no idea what I was supposed to think. I presumed I was about to be given the traditional reveal, the one that happened just before the traditional execution.

"I think I haven't been anywhere or seen anything, and I'll be back in my office without a clue where the last ten hours have gone."

He turned to face me and smiled sadly. This wasn't going well for me. The only thing I was likely to get out of this was the truth, and that was scant compensation for being dead.

"You have something of ours, I believe?"

Years of dealing with money hadn't prepared me for the fact that I was going to die because of someone else's theft.

"If you'd waited another fifteen minutes, I'd have wired it back to you. I'm an honest man, Mr..."

The boss's smile twitched. It was a nice try, but he wasn't giving out freebies today. But then he was distracted, as I was, by a sudden deep blue flash from the doohickey in the centre of the dome.

"Cherenkov radiation, Mr Harrison. Caused by faster-than-light particles interacting with the shielding."

I must have raised an eyebrow or two, because here it came. I guess he didn't often have a chance to explain his operation.

"Time travel, Mr Harrison. Quantum entanglements. Compound interest."

I understood one concept out of the three, so I made a wild leap of logic.

"Are you bringing money back through time?"

Now his smile was genuine. I'd cracked the case, except I still had no idea what had happened to Rached.

"Yes we are, Mr Harrison. We're depositing money in the present, and retrieving it from the future. Fifty years in the future. Our agents situated then have one half of a pair of entangled particles, and we have the other half now. We call forward from here and pair them up again, and we have a decades-long investment in a matter of weeks."

That was cute. It didn't even sound illegal, since it was their money all the way through, no matter how unorthodox the other arrangements were. I could worry about hyperinflation later. Which was, of course, exactly what IR were worrying about now. The technology was, literally, a licence to print money. If everyone was in on it, the markets would collapse with an almighty bang and never recover. Secrecy was paramount.

"All these people..." I circled my finger in the air in front of me.

"Will become our agents in the future. Where Dr Rached is currently, safe and sound. When he decided to help himself to one of our accounts, we had to take action. Fortunately, the entanglement works both ways."

Rached wasn't dead. He was marooned, fifty years in the future by a company who didn't believe in murder.

"And that's what you're going to do to me, right?"

The boss nodded, and I found myself momentarily

thinking that this actually wasn't so bad, that plying my trade half a century from now would be kind of interesting, and I'd still be young enough to enjoy it. So I started looking for the catch.

"When you get there," he said, "you'll find that we own everyone and everything, so there's no one to tell your secret to. But it's not so bad. We're all decent people. Our future is better than you'd expect."

I sensed movement behind me, and there were two different heavies in jumpsuits. One held a taser, the other a glass of water and a pill. On closer inspection, the pill was a tiny magnetic containment vessel with an entangled particle inside, and the water was really flat and tasteless. What else could I do? If I didn't swallow voluntarily, they'd hold me down until I did. I wondered how they'd got it into Rached, and supposed they'd tricked him somehow, with a story about access to facilities or the staff canteen. Hell, maybe they all had them, the ultimate insurance against spies, thieves and whistleblowers.

"You got one?" I cleared my throat. The pill was bigger than the usual painkillers I chowed down on.

"It's a shame we have to meet in such circumstances," said the boss. "You'd have been a good fit for IR. Take him to a hab and make sure he stays there until he goes."

And at the moment I'd resigned myself to my fate – no, looking forward to it in a bittersweet kind of way – the dome imploded.

It was a big volume of air to lose, but the three gaping holes in the ceiling were pretty roomy by themselves and more than capable of reducing a breathable atmosphere to a few sparse molecules in under a minute. It didn't help much that the railgun projectiles punched through the thin skin of the dome as if was wet tissue paper, and saved their kinetic energy for the hard targets below.

If there was an evacuation plan, I wasn't part of it. I

was almost instantly abandoned. I had one thought, one chance, and so ran. Back around the circumference of the rapidly-emptying dome, and through the airlock into the hopper that had delivered me. The IR staff were so well drilled that no one thought to stop me, take me along, or even look for me in the chaos of swirling dust and ear-popping vacuum. I put my back to the door and poked the controls. The automatics decided that the air was too thin and started pumping the reserves into the cabin.

I fell to the deck, gasping. I was bleeding from my nose and my ears, my eyes hurt and I could taste copper and flint in my mouth. I wheezed and coughed and burped and moaned, and hoped an embolism wouldn't finish me off. After five minutes of writhing and twisting, I decided I wasn't going to die, and dragged myself into one of the pilot's seats.

The plexiglas canopy afforded expansive views of the assault ships that JAXA had unleashed, together with the rise and fall of the mobile infantry. Far be it for me to suggest that Fujikawa was using my kidnap to close off the possibility of an IR-dominated future, but it was a hell of an excuse. In his position, I'd have done the same.

I watched them flit backwards and forwards for a while. Sometimes the hopper trembled on its legs, but for the most part, it was a silent, deadly ballet of recoilless weaponry and expanding gasses. One reaction-packed warrior arced over to the deep shadow in front of me. If they'd wanted to kill me, a round through the windscreen would have done it. As it was, they didn't. They peered very carefully at me, then raised a heavily insulated mitt, finger and thumb awkwardly curled around to make the 'ok' gesture. I returned it, and they jetted off again.

It might have been Fujikawa himself, but he never subsequently said. Perhaps he was embarrassed at using me like an ace to trump IR's hand. I was rescued later, when everything had died down. Infinite Resources was no longer a player, and that was pretty much that.

Except that it wasn't. I was left with explaining to Leila what had happened to her husband. I did the best I could. I waved my arms around a lot and drew some diagrams on my pad of paper. In fifty years' time, she'd be an old woman who'd lived through fifty long years, while for him, it would be a blink of an eye. Would he have already tried to find her? She might not even be alive in fifty years, and he'd be left holding a little pot of ashes, or running his finger along her name on a memorial plaque.

"What are you going to do?" I asked her.

She looked lost. Rached had made one mistake. Just one. I couldn't help feeling sorry for him even while I was wanting to smack him around the head for leaving his wife all alone in the past.

"I don't know. There's nothing I can do, is there? Except wait."

There was one thing. It might not work now that IR's facility had been destroyed. Perhaps the machinery still existed in the future, or had been rebuilt, or whatever. Paradoxes weren't my problem. I slid the little magnetic capsule across the table towards her, still warm from my insides from which it had been cut only an hour earlier.

"If they call for me, and get you instead? It's worth a shot, right?"

She took it there and then, gobbled it down like she was starving. The future might not call, but there was always hope.

"Thank you, Mr Harrison. Thank you for everything."

I never saw her again.

Silent in her Vastness

James Worrad

Aiden Adley is the only human being in a twenty mile radius of the University of California, San Diego. He prefers it that way.

Adley drags a featureless mannequin across campus, across a sun-baked square overlooked on all sides by the buildings of the engineering department. He's shifted eight mannequins in the last hour, searching for an effect that a hundred hands couldn't achieve and only one set of eyes can ever hope to appreciate.

Fuck, does he sweat. The square is a baking tray.

All the mannequin, including this one, are anatomically proportionate despite their lack of feature. Their outer layer is a substance that is not skin but will behave exactly like skin – he's reliably informed – in the required moment. Poly-something or other. It feels nothing like skin, though.

Adley's tablet rings in his back pocket.

"Huh."

He stands the mannequin up in the middle of the path, takes his tablet from his pocket and unrolls it. Marcy, his agent. He wipes sweat from his forehead and answers.

"Hey."

She's got that look again.

"Wake up, you limey prick," Marcy says. "What's taking so long? The Chinks are spitting noodle at me here."

"You're being racist, Marcy."

"You're being retarded." Marcy shakes her head and her braids swing in order like a Nuremberg march. "Get on the i-chopper. Now."

"Soon. Just… you sure it's safe?"

"What? Compared to staying there? Jesus, Adley!"

Adley has work to finish and barely enough time. Things burn at his mind here, his memory. Besides, he's in a mood to be alone. Or with a crowd. One-on-one never sits right with him.

"Marcy, listen to me; I'm the artist here. China's the hand, you are the handle – diligently keeping me together – and I am the brush-its-fucking-self." He tries to meet her eyes, but somehow it's too much. "This is as big as it gets, Mar. Installation art's Notre Dame. I won't get another chance to do this right." Hot sun biting down on him. Keeping this up is difficult. "Besides, there's still twenty-three hours to go." He smiles.

Marcy blinks. "Shit, whatever. Not only did you Brits oppress the world, now you want to crack *my* balls, too."

"We prefer 'bollocks'. Back in eight hours, yeah? Twelve tops."

"How you cocksuckers had an Emp –"

"Bye, Marcy." Adley switches off. His smile vanishes. Talking to Marcy – anyone – drains him. This is no time or place for language, for wearing tattered masks.

Concrete buildings on all sides. Beautiful concrete – as it should be – with walls and arches rising from some giant's dream. How could concrete, Adley wonders, ever have failed? So malleable, so willing to indulge humanity's most untamed visions. Outside academic utopias, in the real world, all we can think to make with it are boxes.

Adley only has to stumble a little further. He stands the mannequin against the Department of Magnetic Engineering, presumably emptied of magnets back in the academic crash of '32. First he positions its limbs as if hailing a cab, but the result looks oddly fascist. Instead he alters the arms to appear as if the mannequin is reading the time from one of those wristwatches his parents' generation still wears.

That'll do.

Aidan Adley is being paid to make art for the planet's

foremost nation to enjoy, the most populous too. Famously so. Yet, unbeknownst to his Chinese patrons and the world at large, he also works for an audience of one.

That's how arts supposed to work isn't it? Lots of layers? Well here there's two – the World and himself. Nothing in-between.

Cloudaccount open:

Private note 1: *Sometimes you would walk her home from college instead of taking separate buses. You would walk along the Soar – that bastard hybrid of canal and river bifurcating Leicester city – up to the back of her council house off Belgrave Road.*

There was a little bridge crossing the river just before her home; a curve of wrought iron and tar-coated wood. Faux-middle England twee, Tess of the D'Urbervilles adrift in Hobbiton. And all around it, the river's true landscape – roofless industrial units, desiccated car chassis' and yellow foam on still water. Laughable. The pair of you would laugh.

You called it the Bridge of Secrets. It was a game, a silly thing. The bridge could not be crossed until both of you whispered some secret in the other's ear. About each other, about yourself, the world. It usually ended with laughter and kisses. One time, maybe twice, with shouting. But always, ultimately, with love.

You failed, Adley, failed just like concrete. Ten years gone and no one can recall a single whisper.

SAVE?

Just a tactical nuke. The smallest America ever made: enough to kiss a single Soviet regiment or a battle cruiser at slumber. China can afford to use such a tiny airburst as a printing block and America – God knows – needs the money.

The idea came to Aiden Adley when he read an article about the forthcoming centenary of Hiroshima and

Nagasaki. The blasts had left silhouettes of people on walls and pavements, citizens caught in the glare as they went about their day.

Adley had mentioned the idea on his site, intending it to be mere eyeball-kick, a dark absurdity. He had no nukes, after all, and owned no land save the hundred square feet of marble tiling that was his penthouse in Lagos, 'the Benin Beijing'.

China wasn't Adley. It had everybody's nukes – if only for safety's sake – and more land than it would ever need, including, by way of example, vast squares of unused California.

Like him, Adley thinks as he gazes down from the upper roof of the award-winning Geisel library, China's nascent democracy will find a portrait of its psyche in this installation piece, this victimless ground zero.

The 'South Asian Exchange' of '35 – with its own far larger collection of carbon silhouette-people – had proven a watershed for recently democratic China. They had mounted the greatest humanitarian mission in history (comparable on a logistical scale, it was said, with the eastern front of World War Two) and, in bringing aid to their notional ally Pakistan and their even more notional enemy India, had shed the skin of Tianamen square. A singular superpower – raised to world ascendency on a campaign of mercy.

Adley stares at the wide square below, littered with mannequins. Had they been as oblivious as this in Islamabad and Faisalabad, Mumbai and Jaipur, twenty hours beforehand? Wallahs and software designers, Imams and Bollywood stars, each blind to their end result – charcoal marks on a concrete floor.

He thinks of Rishma Ballal that night she called him. He thinks of her tears and pleading and he winces. He decides to think of other things.

His work here. Yes!

Like China, Aiden Adley finds a likeness of himself in

this piece. His patrons have not paid him for that and neither do they know, but it's there. The campus will be a map of his body, an expression of his life. He has only to define the analogous parts.

Example? The Geisel library, atop its hill, will be his head. Obvious, really. Its mirror glass, multi-layered and futuristic design holds archaic notes and outmoded catalogues. Dusty aluminium shelves.

He pictures it after the blast, the glass but a memory of briefest hot vapour. Tourists in protective suits will marvel, will entertain space operatic fancies – the building's remains some alien skull-monument, a Venusian necropolis of denuded concrete. Silent ruins all around.

Adley spits over the roof wall and on to the larger roof below. The elegance of this self-portrait will be in the fusion of two worlds: his own self (rendered in campus architecture) and the crowds and social groups he has known (symbolised by the many mannequins and their frozen actions).   Adley has come to realise his life has been a film shot in close-ups and wide screen and very little in between. A man happy alone, to think and work alone, and happy in crowds, whether a group of close friends or a hall packed with admirers and press. What he can't do is one-on-one, eye-to-eye. Relationships, basically.

Besides one anomaly – and he doesn't want to think of Rishma Ballal now, he has made enough notes in his cloudaccount today – his private life has been a decade of three-month-fiascos, pity-fucks and missed connections; a breeze of soft skin forever streaming over the horizon. Beyond grasp.

And no one to blame but himself. 'Don't stick your dick in crazy', a friend had once told him; something Adley was prone to do. Good advice that ran both ways. Don't wrap your pussy around it either.

There's a tiled path that leads down from the Geisel library. It's in the shape of a snake uncoiling. The campus planners of yestercentury were riffing on Milton here; blasting out lit-fic power chords of lost innocence and forbidden knowledge. Sadistic bastards, Adley thinks. What a weight to drop on young minds.

He wonders what part of his anatomy the serpent path is. His tongue, perhaps? It rolls straight out of his Geisel-brain, after all. Yet by that same logic it could just as easily be his dick. He decides the path is a synthesis of both.

"White man screw with forked tongue," he mumbles in a movie-Sioux accent. He laughs and screams it to the sky.

Cloudaccount open:

Private Note 2: *One Summer afternoon you ducked out of college together. You found no one at home and had sex on the bed where once you were told bedtime stories, though you never thought of that until years later. Her nudity was still fresh to you then, Adley. All women's bodies were, remember?*

After, you talked; for that's what lovers do on television and neither of you had a better reference. Your skin stuck together and you smelt of each other, which were things telly had never mentioned.

You asked about her make-up and she showed you her bag of alien artifacts: eyeliner, blusher, mascara and lipstick.

She lay on her back and you began to decorate her. First, you made outlines in black eyeliner across her brown skin. Colour next. Her breasts became blossoms of rouge, her belly a hummingbird, mascara wings flashing metallic-green.

More. Thighs of creeping ivy, her pubic hair tinder to a cosmetic flame.

She was a perfect canvas, so still. Occasionally, she would reach out and pet your famished erection, an act that goaded you to paint more, paint truer. She liked that; the power of it. She told you as much and laughed.

She liked you because you could do things she could never hope to do – hold a room of people with a notion clothed in words and, so you always claimed, be entirely happy alone. But she loved you for your unspoken effort, your struggle with the role of boyfriend. And your failure to comprehend all that role entailed.

The make-up got smeared across the bedclothes soon enough. But before that, Adley, you had decided. You were an artist.

SAVE?

As night falls it occurs once more to Aiden Adley that this art piece will not be entirely victimless. Here are hummingbirds, skunks, ravens and bees (happy little bees!), June bugs, lizards and trees. Ignorant, blind to the blast. Casualties in the path of a replica history.

He justifies the deaths, reluctantly, with the cold fact that no work of art is ever perfect and that – if such a work could exist – it would be all artists' duty to destroy it.

Adley has set up his old, much-loved projector on top of the campus bookstore. Its cone of vanilla light falls upon the food court below. The food court, without question, is Adley's bowels and intestinal tract. Gut feeling made concrete.

Images of Nagasaki burns-patients are stretched and warped across grey slabs, metal dinner tables and ambivalent mannequins. Adley only has to thumb a button and monochrome switches to hi-res colour: a girl from a Mumbai suburb, sari patterns seared to her flesh. A young Chinese soldier behind holding her up. What an image – a Pulitzer-winning *pieta*. Another thumb twitch and the food court is lit in the X-ray tones of Adley's dental records. Fillings hunkered down in translucent calcium and flesh. His skull looks like the Geisel library once the nuke has said its piece.

Adley struck lucky earlier. He found a box of old wristwatches in a shop storeroom. He'd thought to place them on the foreheads of mannequins, like bindis, but this seemed overwrought and biased to one side of the South Asian Exchange. Instead, he set their hands to the estimated time of the blast. Then he smashed their faces with a hammer and littered them about the food court's floor. They shine in the projector's light, motes gleaming in the campus' digestive system.

His agent Marcy will be fuming, but he has work to do. He will call her tomorrow morning but for now he's switched off all calls to his tablet. Cloudaccount notes only. Everyone has a cloudaccount now.

Perhaps Rishma Ballal does too. He can never find her on any social media and wouldn't know what to do next if he could. He's only located her online once: a site for actors. Unlike Adley, she hasn't aged a bit. On the site, she reads a children's book to the camera (held by someone credited as Mark Howell); *Three Little Pigs*. What's the significance? Why would anyone make that their only internet appearance? How is that kind of control even possible these days?

He has a slide of that; a still image from her performance. He decides not to put it in the projector though. Not here, not in his bowels.

He flicks his thumb and there's an image from his breakthrough piece – *Below Above*. *Below Above* was based on Bernini's sculpture, *The Ecstasy St Teresa*. Buenos Hamasaki – third generation of a family of Japanese porn stars – posed as the eponymous Carmelite nun. Hamasaki's expression mid-climax, Adley told web-journalists, was exactly that of the enraptured Saint's. The head of the angel above, whose spear had pierced her chest, had been replaced with an old Apple Mac.

He'd made his guests (the London crowd mainly, plus a smattering of Brazilian and Nigerian jet set) laugh and take another glass of boxed wine. When they asked about significance and theme Adley explained that he wasn't what you might call a... *conscious* artist. He just trusted his subconscious and thus far it had kept up with the rent.

Now, atop a derelict bookstore, he wonders what exactly he had sought in *Below Above*. An equilibrium, perhaps; some unseen Lagrange point between Jpeg labia and marble divinity. A simulacrum of love.

Cloudaccount open:

Private notes 3: *The night of the South Asian Exchange she called you from Leicester. Audio only. She had family near Jaipur. She kept crying.*

You were running a three-week workshop in Cornwall, a promising artist dispensing insight. Your rich-kid students were drinking in the common room and watching the news on their tablets. They needed you in there. They needed context. You wanted to go to them and away from her, away from the call. Because, well… why because? Immaturity? Fear? Or was it as you'd said to her; that you were miscast, constantly feeling as if you had taken someone else's role. 'Boyfriend', 'lover'. Her voice trembled and you pretended to listen and she knew and you were relieved when it ended. You could breathe.

Later, she flew to India to help the Chinese aid effort. At about the same time you paid a porn star to be a saint and got an award.

And something neither of you ever named faded into background radiation.

SAVE?

Aiden Adley has time enough yet. Its only early morning and he's still not sure what part of him exactly these trees he stands among represent.

This being America, the good ol' USA, he has found a gun. A shotgun, with a box of many shells. Kept in a locker in the literature department. Go figure.

But this is wonderful serendipity. He's long nurtured a concept involving small arms, but it's nigh-impossible to get a weapons license back in Nigeria. Time, now, for a practice run both jolly and furtive.

This morning he wears nothing but a medical scrubs top and a pair of Ray Bans, both of which he found… Adley can't recall where exactly. On campus, anyway. He has earphones, and an antique iPod weighing down his scrubs breast pocket. He has it set to skip repeatedly from *Herman's Hermits* to *Anal Cunt*. Nothing in-between.

All around him the trees. Anorexic-thin trees in lines, intended so by Campus planners. A rank and file forest standing to order like a third world militia high on coke cut with gunpowder. He read about that in an article; child soldiers of the Newfoundland Liberation Army.

Adley has taped paint cans to a trunk. So many colours.

He puts the gun's stock against his shoulder. Adley's never fired one before, not even an airgun. He's gone so stiff he's shaking. He sweats. He pulls the tri –

The world roars. Adley's back collides with the dusty ground. His shoulder feels as if it's been under a giant staple gun. He yells. He laughs. He gets back on his feet.

The paint tin he was aiming for remains untouched.

Adley tries again. Instinct flinches in him, but he mentally commands his shoulder to brace itself once more. First times the worst.

A lie, he realises as the shotgun kicks. The paint can explodes like a deathstar full of blood. Wonderful.

"Yes! Yes!" Adley barks, teeth gritted. He readies himself and shoots the can below. A blast of blue.

"Take it! Ha! Fuckin' take iiiit!"

Yummy, yummy, yummy, I've got love in my tummy, says the iPod, *Hitler was a sensitive man.*

Adley takes aim once more, but the tree begins to creak and lean toward him.

"Shit."

He dodges the trunk and the heavier branches, gets whipped by a hundred twigs. Screaming, laughing, he runs through the pre-planned wood, Californian breeze caressing his naked thighs.

Here is him, from concrete to glass to mannequin. He runs through himself, is king of all around. And, hyperventilating, he sees that it is good.

He slows and drops to his knees. Closes his eyes and takes deep breath. He can hear the calls of animals and birds, the soon-vaporised wildlife of UCSD campus. Odd, he thinks, that it has not overgrown. Someone must have been mowing and watering and keeping things clean here, ready for his masterpiece.

He sees a hummingbird, its wings metallic green.

Good God, Adley thinks. The hummingbird drinks from a red bloom, then another.

Adley's spine freezes under the Californian sun. He remembers Rishma's body, her honey-brown canvas that he daubed upon one summer afternoon. He realises this image, this vision from a lost bedroom, has been under the surface of his mind all the time he has been here. He is not what you might call a... *conscious* artist.

Adley claws at the dry and paper-light soil. He growls at nothing but earth, bares his teeth to the dead twigs that coat it. He falls on one side, curls up and weeps.

An hour of this passes, then Adley drags a mannequin across campus. He has difficulty carrying the thing up the stairs to the roof of the Oceanview Terrace cafeteria, but eventually manages. The i-chopper, its blades kissed by the morning sun, is sat up there. Adley places the mannequin in one of the seats, then presses 'go' on the chopper's dashboard.

Crouching in the downdraft, he watches the i-chopper ascend, watches it fly along the coast toward San Diego and off, over Tijuana and on to the sanity of populated Mexico. Marcy will be happy to hear it's in the air, at least. He smashes his tablet and takes the stairs down.

Cloudaccount open:

Private note 4: *They never worked out which shadow you were. You are lost among the Hiroshima people, Adley, an unidentified charcoal sketch. I've seen you, though, because I've walked through your final work and made sure to locate every burnt silhouette.*

The Chinese located me after unlocking your Cloudaccount. Two sentences were all that were in it: one some nonsense about concrete failing and the other my name. They've asked me to write something. And so I've made these notes.

But words are just fossils, imprints of feeling.

My sweet disintegrated boy. Sometimes, in bed, I feel a hummingbird upon my belly.

SAVE?

DELETE ALL

On campus there is a statue of a woman on top of a pillar. It used to be a fountain but has long been dry. Adley sits at its base. He is not the campus. Never was. The campus is her; Rishma Ballal. Everything has always, *always*, been her.

Aiden Adley closes his eyes and draws his knees to his chest. Silent in her vastness, he waits for the blast and for their bodies to fuse.

Grief Stricken

Paul Kane

There he is, Lomax's quarry.

The man chats, flirts with members of staff; hasn't the faintest idea what's waiting for him. Lomax grunts – he'll wipe that look of smug satisfaction off the prick's face. One way or another, that bastard will come to grief.

Images fill Lomax's mind: the cutting of skin; flesh parting; blood spurting and pooling, organs being sliced into, removed.

The man finishes his conversation with his female co-workers, who fawn in front of him, giggling like schoolgirls, pushing back strands of hair over their ears – might as well be sucking his cock right there and then in the corridor, in front of everyone. The man laughs too; Lomax fucking hates that. What right does he have to be happy? What right does anyone?

"Can I help you, sir?" Lomax is startled by the question, didn't hear anyone come up behind him, beside him. *You're meant to be a hunter, what the fuck?* He was too focussed on the object of his pursuit. He turns to face her, and she reminds him so much of... Lomax shakes his head, more to clear his mind than to answer her question. But she can't help him. Nobody can, not even God or the Devil or anything in-between. Not anymore. "Only you look a little... Lost."

He *is* lost. He has been for some time. But there's nothing this woman can do about it. Only he can do that, work through things – follow this to its logical conclusion. Only then can he find some sort of release.

Lomax knows he has to say something, but isn't sure what. He manages, "I'm fine, thanks." It's clear he is far from fine.

"Only you were –"

"I said I'm *fine!*" he snaps, and the woman takes a step back.

Don't give yourself away. Don't let her see what you're really here for, what your purpose is, Lomax tells himself. He smiles awkwardly. "I'm sorry, it's been a long day. Long week, in fact. I'm here... you know, visiting someone."

The woman nods her understanding. She's seen all kinds of ways of handling this stuff, of dealing with such heightened emotional states – though not his, he can guarantee that. She won't have seen Lomax's way. It's unique. She leaves him alone, though, so his ploy has worked. He turns back, looks over at the space he'd been scrutinising. The man is gone.

Shit!

Lomax moves forward, his long coat flapping behind him like a superhero. He is anything but. Can't leap tall buildings or dodge bullets, or... or turn back time by flying round the Earth. But he can do one thing, and he does it well. He's a hunter, he finds people. He's been doing it all his life. So find *him;* find the man you're chasing.

The man you're going to kill today.

Christ... Where the fuck has he –

Then Lomax spots him, just a head bobbing down the corridor, but distinctive: that curly brown hair, greying just slightly. That bouncy stride of his, as if he's walking on air. As if he doesn't have a care in the world. He will soon, Lomax will see to that.

I am the bringer of grief.

He pushes past staff and visitors alike. Past the women that man had been flirting with, in their tight, blue and white uniforms. There will be no more of that after today, no more. Lomax will see to it.

He races past nauseating turquoise walls, past wards filled with patients, and spots his prey pressing the button for the lift. *Come on, come on...*

No: Lomax is too late. The metal doors are closing again before he can reach them. But he knows where the man is heading, same place he always does after work. It's just a question of how many stops that lift will make on its way down, how fast Lomax is taking the stairs. Very fast, he has to be. He's decided that he's not going to wait any longer, that the deed has to be done today.

Flinging open the set of double doors, he hurls himself down those steps, two, three at a time. The rational part of his mind is yelling: *slow down, you could fall and injure yourself* (he's in the right place to get fixed up though, isn't he; problem is, he's also in the right place to get flagged, to get noticed by the authorities, and that's the last thing he needs, not when he is so close).

The irrational part is saying: *fuck it.*

Should have lain in wait down there, but he'd had to be sure. Needed to know for certain his prey was in the hospital itself. *Just because his car is...*

Down, down and down. Below the hospital itself, underneath. The staff car park, so dark and full of shadows, no matter how many panels of strip lighting they scatter about the place. Lomax feels at home here – he knows the layout, after scoping it out on several occasions. Knows where the CCTV cameras are. Knows also that if he pulls up the hood on his sweatshirt and angles his head just right, he can avoid detection, avoid identification.

He fights to control his breathing as he hits the basement level. He's going to need it to be even anyway, for what comes next. There's no room for excitement, for adrenalin. Lomax has to be cool and calm now and –

The blood again, the slices: peeling back skin, sinking the knife further inside. The scars that will be left behind afterward, ugly and ragged. The tears stitched together like Frankenstein's monster. The work of uncaring, unfeeling hands.

No, concentrate. You're in the moment.

First things first, he needs to work out how far ahead his quarry is. The lift's bought the guy some time, but Lomax was quick descending those stairs. He keeps himself fit, you see. Has to, it's the only way to do what needs to be done, fuelled by…

Over there, on his way across the car park. There's no mistaking that confident swagger, coat over one arm. That fucking grin. Lomax moves silently across the concrete, flitting between the vehicles – passing 4x4s and people carriers and sports cars – using them for cover, without ever looking like he is. It's a skill: partly practised, partly organic. And soon he isn't very far away from the man at all, which is good, because already the target has his keys out, is depressing the button on them with a *bee-beep*. The orange sidelights of the sleek, silver Jaguar XF flash on and off momentarily. If Lomax is to make his move, it has to be soon.

Has to be *now*.

He darts between bays, rising and gliding forward at the same time. One hand reaching under his coat.

"Hey… Hey you!" As before, the voice breaks his concentration, and he turns to see a figure heading his way. "What are you up to there, eh?" Once again, he has failed to spot this person creeping up on him – that's supposed to be Lomax's job, the creeping – because he was so intent on what he was going to do. So blinkered that…

His prey is turning as well, closer than the interloper to Lomax. Close enough to see what Lomax's hand is resting on at his belt, and panic. The other man, the figure running over towards him, is closing the gap. Lomax sees that he is also wearing a uniform. Not hospital staff: security. And his baton pretty much drawn. This really isn't good.

His prey is backing up towards the Jaguar, turning and fumbling with the door handle. He'll escape if Lomax isn't careful. *If you'd been more careful in the first place…* he says to himself, but doesn't finish the sentence.

Lomax sighs, and rushes towards the security guard.

He avoids the baton swing, ducking and coming up again in a single, smooth movement, arm out straight, catching the man – solidly built, but terrible reactions – across the bridge of the nose. It explodes in a fountain of blood. The security man scrunches up his eyes. Lomax knees him in the stomach, crumpling him over; the baton falls from his grasp, clattering on the concrete. They're attracting too much attention, Lomax knows that. This needs to be finished, and quickly. One more blow to the back of the head ensures that the guard isn't getting up again any time soon.

Then it's back to the original focus of his attentions. Covering the distance in a couple of strides, reaching inside his coat, drawing the gun and aiming. The driver's door is now shut, though – the engine of the Jaguar being gunned. Lomax skirts the vehicle, trying the door and hoping against hope the bastard hasn't had time to lock them after him yet.

Click! He hasn't... Lomax yanks open the door, but the man's ready, fear driving him. He lashes out, knocking the pistol from Lomax's grasp. Then he pushes Lomax back and into the neighbouring car. The glass of the passenger window cracks as Lomax connects with it. He lets out a grunt – not of disgust now, but because of the pain in his back.

His quarry has barged past him, just as Lomax did with the people in the corridor. But Lomax is quick to recover, always has been. He's on the guy in seconds, leaping and toppling him, bringing him to the ground with a rugby tackle. But the man still isn't going down without a fight; not that Lomax would have expected anything less. The man kicks out a foot, ramming it into Lomax's shoulder. It's enough to set him free again, and he's crawling away.

Enough of this shit! Lomax gets to his feet, walks calmly back to the Jaguar and picks up his pistol. The quarry has also regained his footing and is stumbling, attempting to run. It doesn't matter. Lomax aims and fires, hitting the man squarely in the centre of the back. He goes down, hard.

It's over.

No, not yet. Now they have to get out of there before anyone else shows up. Before more people arrive than Lomax can handle. He is only one man after all, even if he is a predator. Lomax holsters his weapon, goes over to his target and plucks out the dart. *How's it feel to be on the receiving end of a needle, fucker?* he thinks to himself. There's no point saying it out loud, the man is unconscious.

Lomax picks him up, carries him to the Jaguar like a best man getting the groom back to his hotel after a stag do. He glances round quickly, then opens the door and deposits his prize on the back seat. He swings into the driver's seat and closes the door.

With the precision of a professional, Lomax reverses the Jag out of the tight spot, manoeuvres it around, and drives up and out of this section. He looks into the rear view only once as he makes his way out of the car park, up and into the world above.

But he fails to see the vehicle pull out of its own space just moments after him.

Fails to see the dark green Ford that follows.

As Lomax finishes strapping down the naked man to the cold, metallic surface, he allows himself a half-smile, though it is tinged with pain. *Finally*, he thinks. *Finally*.

Then he thinks about all the things he has planned, what he's going to do. Start with an incision down the middle, probably. He sees the flesh parting again, the blood. There will be so much blood. So much... grief.

The man's eyelids are flickering. He'll be waking up from the drug soon enough. Lomax has gagged him, not because he doesn't want to hear his pleas for mercy or his screams – those would be so sweet. But because he doesn't want to hear his excuses. He's heard far too many of those.

Lomax taps his knife against his lips. With the man laid out in front of him here, he can't help musing about the events that set him down this path.

Did they turn him *into* what he is? Perhaps. But don't they also say that the capacity to kill is either in you or it isn't? That no matter what the trigger is, some people act, while others don't. How can anyone say *how* they'll react to a certain set of circumstances unless they are in them? It's impossible. It's like...

Like being in love.

You know how you think you'll act, but nothing prepares you for that bolt out of the blue. Or how it will change your life forever. The loss of it changes you too, Lomax knows that. It's as much of an adjustment, though infinitely less pleasant it has to be said.

Once upon a time, another life ago, Lomax had been in love.

It is better to have loved and lost...

Lost, so lost. So long ago.

He'd been married, in fact, his wedding anniversary the 24th March. His wife, Tracey, knew what he did – and though she didn't like it, she tolerated it. She knew this was what he was good at. Being a hunter.

John Lomax. Detective John Lomax.

Deep down, he knew she also respected him for bringing people to justice. Catching murders and rapists. Lomax never thought he'd be tracking down his wife's killer. Never thought he'd be doing it alone, either, without the support of his former colleagues. But then, if Tracey hadn't gone in for that surgery...

Minor, they'd said; a routine operation. His smile turns into a grimace as he looks down on the man below him: the curly-haired doctor with the laugh, with the grin. "It's just routine, she'll be up and on her feet again in no time," he had chirped back then, shaking their hands.

Doctor Brendan Carter, he called himself. In a different hospital, a different city. A different world. A happier place until…

Lomax remembers the time he spent with Tracey before the operation. How scared she'd been then, suddenly – and how right she'd been to be so. "John," she'd said, laying in the bed, chewing her bottom lip, "I have a terrible feeling about this."

Lomax had patted her hand, told her everything was going to be fine. "Trust me," he'd even said. Jesus, how many times did they say that in soaps: everything was going to be all right? It was always the kiss of death. Like saying "I'll be right back" in some cheesy horror movie, before getting your head lopped off.

But the trust she'd placed in him, the trust Lomax had placed in the doctors – in Carter especially – had been very misplaced indeed.

Lomax fights back the tears, as he recalls waiting in that corridor; thinking that this was taking a long time, longer than they'd said it would. Remembers seeing staff rushing to and fro, as if to answer some emergency but assuming: they're for someone else, it's a big place, there are more patients than Tracey having ops. But he'd known, even as they emerged through those double doors, even before Carter could say a word, that she was gone.

"We did everything we could," intoned the curly-haired man, though was there just a slight trace of a smile playing on those lips? And was he – *yes*, checking out those nurses in the corridor, in their tight blue and white uniforms. For fuck's sake! "There were… certain complications."

"What kind of complications?" Lomax had demanded, feeling oddly detached, as if he were having an out of body experience (aren't they supposed to be reserved for people actually under the knife?). It was as if he wasn't even there, like he *was* watching this on some stupid soap.

Carter spouted a load of medical jargon about internal

bleeding and trying to trace the problem, though in the end it amounted to one thing and one thing only: they screwed up and now he was a widower. Tracey had been his everything, and now he had nothing.

Nothing except trying to get to the truth, trying to get her justice.

Lomax had insisted on an investigation, which the hospital said they'd conduct internally. Lawyers were brought in, but they were less than useless. In the end Lomax went down to the morgue and broke in, examined the body himself, which was still on ice because of all the fuss he'd kicked up. He'd wept over her cold form as he saw all the cuts, the rough patchwork of stitches that made up her body (they later tried to tell him it was because of the 'further work' they'd done to fully determine cause of death – work that had been conducted *because* of Lomax's questions). But that had just earned him a reprimand, and meant that the ongoing investigation would now be shut down. His Super had even suggested taking some time off, that he was too close to all this.

"You've got to believe me," he said to his partner Trent, a strapping ex-Marine who'd joined the force after injuring his leg on some foreign battlefield. "There's something more going on here. A cover up, I don't know."

Trent trusted him, the kind of trust Carter couldn't begin to understand. They'd worked together for a long, long time and on a number of cases – some of them quite high profile, such as catching the train track killer – always had each other's backs. In fact, Lomax had even taken a bullet for Trent on one occasion, something he reminded him of then. So Trent agreed to help look into all this, on their own time. "You have a sense about these things," Trent had told him. "I've always envied that."

And he had – Lomax had always possessed a flair for thinking outside the box when it came to criminal behaviour. (*Takes a killer to track a killer...* isn't that so?)

Something about this whole thing, about Carter in particular, didn't sit right. He and Trent had conducted their own private investigation, fitted in around the cases they had on their desks. And guess what? More suspicious deaths had cropped up, linked to Carter, who had used a variety of different names in the past. "This is it," Lomax had said to his friend. "This is all the evidence we need." He would finally get justice for Tracey. But they'd been dismissed again, told to drop it – Lomax ordered to take some personal time.

Then, lo and behold, Lomax discovered that Carter had done a runner. Nobody had seen him for a fortnight. So, he'd taken that holiday. Taken that and more besides, and gone after his wife's killer. The man had obviously been doing this a long time, courtesy of the perfect cover – everyone trusts a doctor, they do all that they can (well, what if they did a few things they shouldn't? played God with death as well as life?). And he would continue doing this unless Lomax found him and put a stop to things.

It had taken a while. Taken all of Lomax's detective skills, his tracking abilities, to find the man – now posing as one Doctor Gerry Young – and now he would make him pay. Lomax would cause him so much grief, transfer it onto him and maybe then he'd finally be able to find peace. For him and for Tracey.

Lomax hears the man on the table stirring, his muffled groans through the gag. "Ah, you're awake," he says, leaning over him. "Hello again, Doctor 'Carter'. Remember me?"

The man thrashes about, but he's held tight by his bonds. He's going nowhere.

Lomax sweeps a hand behind him, drawing attention to their surroundings: an abandoned warehouse he found down by the docks. The perfect place for a little privacy. "What do you think?"

The man mumbles something and Lomax laughs softly, holds up the knife, which glints in the light from a portable lamp. "This is my operating theatre, Doctor. *My* theatre of pain." Then he goes on to relate all the things he's intending to do, getting justice for poor Tracey. No, getting *revenge!* Even as he's saying them, Lomax realises how sick it all sounds, but he doesn't care. This is the only way: the one, sure-fire way, he's going to assuage these feelings.

"I'm afraid I can't let you do that, Johnny," comes a voice, echoing through the warehouse. Lomax stands stock-still. For the third time today, he's let someone get the drop on him. Getting old... old and tired.

Third time's the charm, though – right? And he recognises that voice.

"Trent," he says, under his breath.

"Long time no see, Johnny. You didn't write, you didn't call..."

Lomax turns, faces the large man striding across the warehouse floor, half in shadow. He cuts an imposing figure, Trent. Shoulders like breezeblocks, arms like iron girders.

"Walk away, Lewis, this doesn't concern you."

Trent sighs. "I'm afraid it does. I can't let you kill an innocent man, Johnny."

"Innocent?" Lomax spits out the word like snake venom he's sucked from a wound. "How can you say that? This fucker killed my Tracey." He nods at his captive.

"No... No, he didn't."

Lomax looks from the strapped down man to Trent. "What are you talking about? You saw the evidence, same as I did."

"There *was* no evidence, John. Deaths, yes – but not down to Carter. Different doctors in different hospitals. All accidents, all due to negligence or human error, but not done on purpose. Just part and parcel of the risks you take when you have surgery, that's all. Just stupid, bad luck. Like what happened to Tracey..."

"No!" he screams. "You're lying. Why are you lying?

Did they get to you?"

"Who, John?"

"The people who covered it all up?"

Another sigh. "There are no people, John. There's no Carter anymore, either."

"No, I know. He's calling himself Young, now. He's there Lewis, right there. He ran away, but I found him."

Trent continues walking towards Lomax. "Carter's dead. You killed him, remember?"

No, not yet. But I'm going to, Lomax says to himself.

"It's the grief, John. That's what did this to you... Can't you see that? You have to trust me. "

Trust...

Can't you see? Lomax takes another look at the man in front of him, the curly hair – no, it's straight... Straight hair...

"I can't let you kill another one. Not another innocent man. Not now I've finally found you after all these years."

Lomax almost laughs out loud at that one. The hunter being hunted himself, and by his ex-partner.

Not like the rest... Not like the rest... All these years, all these years... The words echo in his mind, just as they did in the abandoned warehouse. He blinks, and the man's face changes – he sees face after face, in fact. All the people he's murdered. Lomax shakes his head. No, they were all Carter, using pseudonyms.

"Put the knife down, Johnny," says Trent, coming closer.

"I... No, I'm not going to do that," Lomax tells him, then sees what Trent has in his hand. It's not a dart gun, this one: it's real. It'll hurt. But can he kill his old partner, kill his friend?

Takes a killer to catch a –

"I said drop it, John." There's an edge to Trent's voice, suggesting he's not going to ask twice.

Lomax makes his move, rushing him. There's a bang and he angles himself sideways. *Whadya know, I can dodge bullets after all,* he thinks. He can do anything in fact, powered by grief like his. Can take on an eighteen stone ex-Marine, for example, by going for his weak spot – the knee – kicking down hard on that and knocking the pistol from his grasp at the same time. And before he knows it, Lomax has plunged the knife he's holding into Trent, forcing it upwards. Trent splutters, warm blood and spittle peppering Lomax's face. He holds his former partner, cradles him as he falls to the floor. He's so heavy Lomax can hardly manage.

"I'm sorry," he whispers, but he doesn't know if Trent can hear his voice. "But I have to finish this. For Tracey."

Once Trent is dead, Lomax returns to the table. To the man he'd once known as Carter. "Now, this is just routine. A minor procedure. You'll be on your feet in no time," Lomax informs him. "Unless there are... complications, of course. But I'll do everything I can." He lets the words sink in, savouring the terrified look on the man's face, in his eyes, the incomprehensible mumbling.

"Trust me," Lomax says, then gets to work.

There he is, Lomax's quarry.

The man chats, flirts with members of staff; hasn't the faintest idea what's waiting for him. Lomax grunts – he'll wipe that look of smug satisfaction off the prick's face.

One way or another, that bastard will come to grief...

The (De)Composition of Evidence

Alex Dally MacFarlane

From: patty.hu@gmail.com
To: nate.leatham@sussex.pnn.police.uk

Unable to cross the border while carrying four pieces of human skin – visa issue. Not a bit of interest in my bag beyond the usual X-ray. I've been sent to a hotel while the matter is handled, but with the national holiday and the need to send paper documentation to the nearest city with a suitable consulate, I've been told it'll take 10 calendar days. There's no fridge in my hotel room.

From: patty.hu@gmail.com
To: nate.leatham@sussex.pnn.police.uk

The ice I bought has melted and the shops are all shut for the long weekend. The room is stuffy. It stinks. The skin has already started to discolour: mottles stealing letters and whole words, ink bleeding into bruise. I'm storing it in a cool box but I keep looking. Border towns. The bar is dreary.

From: patty.hu@gmail.com
To: nate.leatham@sussex.pnn.police.uk

The mottles and bruising and rot have made new words: removed words and letters, left others that seem to say something. Distorted the handwriting. The story the murderer – our murderer? – was waiting for in the whole story? (See attached photos of the skin when I found it and the skin now.) Necrotic plunderverse. Must be a property of the ink(s) used. I took samples – back on day one, and today, from the remaining words.

What else have you got from our murderer?

From: patty.hu@gmail.com
To: nate.leatham@sussex.pnn.police.uk

Why not tell her what it said?

From: patty.hu@gmail.com
To: nate.leatham@sussex.pnn.police.uk

Weirder still: another layer. Angrier. What does our murderer think? Is it the story she wanted?

I'll get your reply on the other side of the border. My passport was returned half an hour ago and I'm standing in the queue to cross.

From: patty.hu@gmail.com
To: nate.leatham@sussex.pnn.police.uk

Below I've written a draft of my report. Let me know if you'd like anything added/removed.

REPORT: THE SKIN OF AN MACLEOD (THE BONE GALL GROUP)
PRIVATE INVESTIGATOR PATTY HU

3 January 2018

The arrest of JO MACLEOD immediately upon her arrival in England for her suspected involvement in the series of murders and partial flayings by a group named THE BONE GALL GROUP and her subsequent confession provided a tip to the location of the body of AN MACLEOD: Bishopton in Renfrewshire, Scotland. I crossed the border and reached the address given by JO MACLEOD. In the kitchen freezer, I found four pieces of skin with writing on them: two large, two very small.

I found the rest of the body in the upstairs bathroom, intact in the bath, with four patches of skin missing: one (large) from the stomach, one (large) from the left thigh and two (smaller) from each forearm. I did not touch the body.

I returned immediately to the border with the four pieces of skin in a cool box, only to face issues with my United Kingdom Permanent Residency that required my passport to be sent to Glasgow. The delay and the lack of refrigeration in my hotel room caused the evidence to decompose.

The complete writing on the four pieces of skin appeared to tell a story, which I have arranged in what I believe to be the correct order.

As it decomposed, the writing began to distort and disappear, until on the fourth day the words and letters formed a second story or message. On the seventh day, the final remaining words and letters again formed a message. I took samples of the ink at all stages of decomposition and took photographs every day.

I learned from DETECTIVE INSPECTOR NATE LEATHAM that JO MACLEOD laughed upon hearing the message of the seventh day.

When my passport was returned to me and I could cross the border, I delivered the pieces of skin to DETECTIVE INSPECTOR NATE LEATHAM. Nothing remained by this time but rot and rank ruin.

DAY ONE

No oral-teller is authorised to say where ink was created. It is not our property. We are not the writers of annals or the holders of yellow-edged folios. Though we use ink to preserve tales in times when speaking aloud is not possible, it is only an act of borrowing.

In turn, they may not tell when the first person opened their mouth to share a tale.

The ink-users permit us this:

A very long time ago, in an undisclosed part of the world, there was an undisclosed woman who we may call Uu, who burnt her sister. To hide the parts of her sister that would not go up in ink-dark smoke, sky-swallowed, Uu ground her bones into a dark powder and mixed it with several undisclosed substances, and on an auroch's shoulder blade she wrote for the first time in ink.

I am a poor oral-teller. If I begin to tell, I trip. I stop. Words worry me. I cannot sing a ballad or a chantry or tell even a humble prologue. I hate it. Stories are easier in silence: indigo ink on my skin. I want to die indigo with stories, letters within letters, opaque. Scan me at a high resolution, magnify, magnify: there, the shades, the words running across my body. I speak better this way.

Listen:

I do not feel guilty telling you this because I took it from an oral-teller. Rule-breaker. My sister. She said:

Uu wrote, in her last year, utterly silent, a great manual of bone-inks. The culmination of a long life. None of it is believed. She wrote numerous chapters: of how fox-bone ink plays tricks on the eye, how manticore-bone ink sings what it says, how salmon-bone ink swims from the next page in search of its birth river. A romance. Yet one thing in this unpublished text interests me: that the bone of sisters inspires the author to make the most beautiful tales.

I am waiting, but all I can tell of is the sound she screamed when I cut off her arm: a plea.

The ink is beautiful.

Wait. Listen.

I want to tell. I want you to listen.

DAY FOUR

No oral-teller: rise! say   ink.   no
rope   no   writers of annals   hold
  y o   u.   n o   tales.
      speaking aloud   is only an act

               l   i st e n   I
   share a tale.
           I :

                       burnt   sister
hid   i   n g   in ink
         bone in   k
          on an auroch's shoulder blade
wrote for the first time

I am a   teller. I   tell
words   I
hum   hate   to   silence:
  my   stories:
      me
              I speak better this way.
Listen:
  Do not feel guilty.   I took
       my sister. She said:
  o   h   utterly silent   bone-ink , the
culmination of a long life– NO.   li   s
  te n!   fox-bone ink plays tricks on the eye,
manticore-bone ink sings   I
s i   n g
      in   unpublished text, I

sister,   a   m   the most beautiful tales.
I am   the sound   screamed when I
          plea.

          Listen.

          I want you to listen.

DAY SEVEN

sister

I

hate
y   o

u
sister
o   h

sister█

scream

plea

I want you to

About the Authors

Jay Caselberg is an Australian author based in Europe. His work has appeared in multiple venues worldwide, and he has a new novel out shortly; as usual, something quite dark. More can be found at http://www.jaycaselberg.com

Emma Coleman has a story forthcoming in PS Publishing's *PostScripts* while her stories "Signals" and "Home" were published by Greyhart and NewCon Presses respectively. The latter gained honourable mention in Ellen Datlow's *Year's Best* and was longlisted for the Bram Stoker Award. Emma states that, among other things, she would find it unpleasant to live without The Professionals, darts, and David Bowie, but could very happily live without adverts, milky tea, and UKIP.

Paul Kane is the award-winning, bestselling author and editor of over forty books – including the sold-out *Hooded Man* (*Arrowhead* trilogy omnibus), *Hellbound Hearts*, *Lunar* (set to be turned into a feature film, scripted by Paul), *Ghosts* and the Y.A. novel *The Rainbow Man* (as P.B. Kane). Find out more about Paul at www.shadow-writer.co.uk.

Alex Dally MacFarlane is a writer, editor and historian. When not researching narrative maps in the legendary traditions of Alexander III of Macedon, she writes stories, to be found in *Clarkesworld Magazine*, *Strange Horizons*, *Heiresses of Russ 2013: The Year's Best Lesbian Speculative Fiction*, and other anthologies. She is the editor of *Aliens: Recent Encounters* (Prime Books, 2013) and *The Mammoth Book of SF Stories by Women* (Constable & Robinson, 2014).

Gateshead-based Dr **Simon Morden** trained as a planetary

geologist, realised he was never going to get into space, and decided to write about it instead. Simon has written eight novels and novellas, and won the Philip K Dick Award for three of them. 2014 sees the arrival of *Arcanum*, a massive (and epic) alternate-history fantasy, which has flaming letters on the cover.

Marie O'Regan is an author and editor whose fiction has appeared in a number of genre magazines and anthologies. She was shortlisted for the British Fantasy Award for Best Short Story in 2006, and Best Anthology in 2010 and 2012. She is co-editor of *Hellbound Hearts, The Mammoth Book of Body Horror* and *A Carnivàle of Horror – Dark Tales from the Fairground*, plus editor of *The Mammoth Book of Ghost Stories by Women*.

Paul Graham Raven is a postgrad researcher in infrastructure futures and theory at the University of Sheffield, as well as a futurist, writer, literary critic and occasional journalist; his work has appeared in such venues as *New Scientist, Wired UK, ARC Magazine* and *The Guardian*. He lives with a duplicitous cat, three guitars he can hardly play, and sufficient books to constitute a fire hazard.

Adam Roberts is the author of fourteen SF novels, including the BSFA- and Campbell Award winning *Jack Glass* (Gollancz 2012) and *Twenty Trillion Leagues Under the Sea* (with Mahendra Singh; Gollancz 2014). He was born in South London and now lives a few miles west of London, so never let it be said that he's averse to travel.

Donna Scott's fiction has been previously published by NewCon, Norilana, Immanion and Pink Narcissus Presses. As well as writing stories she is a freelance editor, blogger, performance poet and stand-up comedian, who has performed all over the UK. Donna is also the Chair of the

British Science Fiction Association. She currently resides in Northampton with her husband and two cats.

E. J. Swift is the author of the novels *Osiris* and *Cataveiro*, the first two volumes in The Osiris Project trilogy. Her short fiction has been published in *Interzone* and in anthologies including *The Best British Fiction 2013* and *Pandemonium: The Lowest Heaven*.

Simon Kurt Unsworth is a prolific writer of supernatural fiction whose short stories have featured in various venues since the mid noughties. Simon's work has been selected for several *Year's Best* anthologies, with "The Church on the Island" shortlisted for the World Fantasy Award in 2008. His most recent collection, *Quiet Houses* (Dark Continent), appeared in 2011.

Paula Wakefield's fiction has appeared in national magazines and short story anthologies. A former journalist, Paula currently teaches professional and creative writing at a Midland university, and is a support worker and trainer for a national bereavement charity. She loves gardening and admits to having been pricked by thorns; thankfully, she's always woken up again.

James Worrad is known for writing fantastic fiction. Armed with ceaseless wit, early Brando good-looks and fearsome intelligence, he is a 2011 graduate of the Clarion Writers' Workshop, UCSD, and his stories have appeared in *Daily Science Fiction*, *Flurb* and the anthology *Burning with Optimism's Flames* (Obverse). Cyber-stalk him at his blog, 'Spool Pidgin': (jamesworrad.blogspot.com).

la femme

The companion volume to *Noir*
Edited by Ian Whates

For anyone who still considers woman to be the weaker
sex… Think again.

Twelve stories of dark science fiction, the supernatural,
blood-rich fantasy, puzzling mysteries and shocking twists
from:

Stephen Palmer, Frances Hardinge, Storm
Constantine, Andrew Hook, Adele Kirby,
Stewart Hotston, John Llewellyn Probert,
Jonathan Oliver, Maura McHugh, Holly Ice,
Ruth Booth, Benjanun Sriduangkaew

www.newconpress.co.uk

Moon Shots

NewCon Press in collaboration with SpaceWitch.

Launched in February 2014, Moon Shots provides a subscription service that delivers a regular fix of top quality short fiction in both e-book and audio format; a new story every two weeks.

Stories will cover the entire gamut of genre fiction, from hard SF to soft SF, from heroic fantasy to urban, dark fantasy to horror, slipstream to the bizarre. Contributors include established authors and exciting new voices coming together to bring you the very best in short fiction.

The first tranche of releases includes original stories from:
Eric Brown, Adam Roberts, Adrian Tchaikovsky, Emma Coleman, Neil Williamson, Rod Rees, Gary Couzens, Esther Saxey and more…

The audio versions are read by a team of narrators that includes a stage and TV actor as well as professional audiobook narrators.

Stories are available individually, but the cost is heavily discounted for a subscription, which covers twelve releases.

Individual story: £1.79 (in e-book and audiobook)
Subscription: £6.99 (as above, 12 stories over approx. 6 months)

Available to buy now at:

http://www.spacewitch.com/moonshots-subscription

"Do you remember that place we used to hang out at, back when every day was drenched in sunshine and the summers seemed to last for ever?"

"God, yes, I'd forgotten about that. We had some fun back then, didn't we? What was it called again, that place?"

"Alice Street."

"Yeah, that's it: Alice Street. Where was it, now?"

"Dunno... Hanged if I can remember..."

Alice Street

Coming soon from NewCon Press
Edited by Tom Hunter

David Barnett
Paul Cornell
Kim Curran
Amy McCulloch
Juliet E McKenna
Lou Morgan
Laure Eve
Adrian Tchaikovsky
Danie Ware
Ian Whates

NEWCON PRESS

Publishing quality Science Fiction, Fantasy, Dark Fantasy and Horror for eight years and counting.

Winner of the 2010 'Best Publisher' Award from the European Science Fiction Society.

Anthologies, novels, short story collections, novellas, paperbacks, hardbacks, signed limited editions, e-books... Why not take a look at some of our other titles?

Neil Gaiman, Brian Aldiss, Kelley Armstrong, Alastair Reynolds, Stephen Baxter, Christopher Priest, Tanith Lee, Joe Abercrombie, Dan Abnett, Nina Allan, Sarah Ash, Neal Asher, Tony Ballantyne, James Barclay, Chris Beckett, Lauren Beukes, Aliette de Bodard, Chaz Brenchley, Keith Brooke, Eric Brown, Pat Cadigan, Jay Caselberg, Michael Cobley, Storm Constantine, Peter Crowther, Hal Duncan, Jaine Fenn, Jonathan Green, Frances Hardinge, Gwyneth Jones, Jon Courtenay Grimwood, M. John Harrison, Amanda Hemingway, Paul Kane, Leigh Kennedy, Kim Lakin-Smith, David Langford, Alison Littlewood, James Lovegrove, Una McCormack, Sophia McDougall, Alex Dally McFarlane Gary McMahon, Ken MacLeod, Ian R MacLeod, Gail Z Martin, Juliet E McKenna, John Meaney, Simon Morden, Mark Morris, Anne Nicholls, Stan Nicholls, Marie O'Regan, Philip Palmer, Stephen Palmer, Sarah Pinborough, Rod Rees, Andy Remic, Mercurio D Rivera, Adam Roberts, Justina Robson, Gaie Sebold, Robert Shearman, Sarah Singleton, Martin Sketchley, Kari Sperring, Benjanun Sriduangkaew, Brian Stapleford, Charles Stross, Tricia Sullivan, EJ Swift, Adrian Tchaikovsky, Steve Rasnic Tem, Lavie Tidhar, Lisa Tuttle, Simon Kurt Unsworth, Ian Watson, Freda Warrington, Liz Williams, Neil Williamson and many more.